The Lady in the Street - T(

& M. A. C

Cover Art by Emmy Elli

All Rights Reserved

THE LADY IN THE STREET

Emmy Ellis

M. A. Comley

PROLOGUE

In the shadows of my mind, there you are,
Mocking and laughing, rejecting me.
One day I'll come for you,
And it will set me free.

The mask of a woman covered his face. It itched. Sweat beaded beneath the rubber. It didn't smell too good and reminded him of Halloween as a kid. Giggling, running through the dark streets, knocking on doors and asking for sweets. Except his mother had never taken him through the streets. He'd had to tag along behind other families, pretending to be one of them.

Those days were gone. Now all he had was the future.

With his hood up and a long blonde wig on, he could pass for a female if no one got too close. An attractive one. Maybe Pamela Anderson in *Baywatch*. His clothes were androgynous, so when he next took the disguise off, he'd be just a man, walking along, minding his own business. After, he'd turn the hoodie inside out, from black to red. For all he knew, people might be out and about when he was on his way home, despite the late hour. If he got seen, they'd remember the red, not some woman head to toe in black.

The scent of the sea wafted to him on a cold breeze, shifting strands of the wig so they sprawled across his mask. The tail end of a hurricane had been imminent for days, so the local weatherman had said. All they'd had today was a bit of manic rain and some high winds that only rustled the tree branches but didn't bend the trunks.

He thought about the recent murders that had been on the news just the other day. Three sisters, killed by their foster brother. It had spurred him on to do what he was doing now after so long planning, of gathering the courage. He had people he wanted to kill, and he reckoned it was about time he got on with it. Too many years had passed with him just thinking.

It was the perfect moment to act.

Making Smaltern a place where tourists didn't want to come would be fun, too. He hated the fucking town and had only stuck around to see justice come to pass.

Most of his future victims would be tucked up in bed by now after a long day at work or propping up the bar of The Villager's Inn—they had a lock-in tonight. One of the dead sisters had worked there. Emma. He'd shagged her a few weeks back. Happy to spread her legs, that one. He'd been happy for her to do it and all.

He glanced at his watch.

Almost time.

He stared at the bedroom window of person number one. Any second now, they'd turn their lamp off. He'd wait five minutes for them to fall asleep, then he'd go inside.

He was glad he'd thought to do it this way, with the long hair and the mask, relics from his childhood.

To all intents and purposes, he was just the lady in the street.

CHAPTER ONE

Felicity longed for sleep. Tonight had been...taxing. Better than calling it a complete fuckup. She'd had a series of dodgy phone calls from the same person, the voice all weird, as though they'd been trying to disguise it. Like she wasn't used to crank callers. She knew when someone was trying hard not to be recognised. She worked for Talk Today, like the Samaritans, every Monday evening, answering the phone in the little office in town above Chargrill Kebabs. It was her way of giving back to those people who needed someone to listen to them. She'd had no one she could tell about her past while it had been going on, so now it was over, if she could give another human being or two an ear, it might balance things out. You know, have her feeling better about herself.

She'd done a few things she wasn't proud of. At least Becky was still her friend, despite Felicity's hideous confession.

Something tapped on the window, and she jumped, stifling a whimper. She'd been on edge the past few days since news of the Walker sisters' murders had been on the telly. All right, the bloke had been caught, but that didn't really lower the fear factor. Not for someone who had fears lurking in every dark corner.

Like her.

What if *they'd* come back for her? What if they'd figured out where she lived?

Straining her ears, she waited for the sound to come again, convincing herself it had been a tree branch scraping across the glass. The weather had been awful today, so it could have been the rain making the racket.

The noise of wind moaning ramped up her unease. It wailed as though a mournful ghost, and she shivered, burying her head under the quilt, her breaths soon warming her up. If she managed to get to sleep this side of midnight, it would be a miracle. She had to be up at eight to get ready in time for her shift to start at Smaltern Amusements.

To calm herself, she thought of the dull day she'd have, listening to the tinkles and tunes blaring out of the various slot machines, and the annoying horn blast if anyone won a teddy from the claw grab. It always managed to have her jumping out of her seat in the coin exchange booth. Bloody thing.

I need to find something else, something with better wages.

Although she didn't have rent or a mortgage to pay, what with Gran dying recently and leaving her this place, she still had the utilities to fork out for. Electricity didn't come cheap, did it, and —

"Fuck, what was that?" she whispered.

Gran's dog, Harlow, yipped from the kitchen. The Yorkshire terrier wouldn't be any good at helping her if anyone broke into the bungalow, and Felicity would swear someone was trying. There it was again, the rattle of a handle being tested.

It couldn't just be the wind.

"God…" She sat up, her breaths unsteady, the quilt slithering down to bunch on her lap. Her body seemed to hollow, and she willed herself to be brave and go into the hallway.

If she padded down it, she'd see if anyone was in the front garden through the glass in the front door. Even though it was mottled with a warped pattern, it'd still show a shape. A lamppost stood on the pavement at the end of her path, so the light would give whoever it was away.

Look through the window now then. Why go to the door?

She ignored that voice, grabbed her phone off the nightstand, and made her way from her bedroom. No shape. No ominous stranger trying to get in. She crept into the living room and peered outside, wishing she'd closed the curtains before she'd gone to bed.

Nothing. Just grass. A hedge.

And a blonde woman with a stark white face staring straight in.

Felicity yelped a bit and stepped to the side, slapping a hand to her chest, her heart ticking too fast and dull, adrenaline flushing her system. She watched from behind the safety of the curtain, but the woman wasn't there now.

"For fuck's sake. Get a bloody grip, will you?" Her whisper came out contorted, wretched.

There hadn't really been a woman. She was seeing things. Imagining people when there weren't any.

That was what *they'd* done to her. She'd never be free of them. Their faces visited her dreams at night, their grins leering, gazes devouring her.

She blew out a nerve-steadying breath and went back to bed. Thoroughly unsettled, she tossed and turned, lying on her side, eventually comfortable, facing away from the window that overlooked the front garden. If there really had been someone there for that brief moment, it had only been a woman, probably on her way home, and she might have stopped walking when she'd spotted Felicity gawping, then carried on her way.

Yes, that was it.

She closed her eyes and listened to her breaths, concentrating so they were the only sounds she zeroed in on. She drifted, sleep coming to call. Harlow yapped again, though, breaking the spell, and Felicity's heartrate skittered.

"This is doing my head in," she muttered.

"Not half as much as it's doing mine."

Oh God. Oh fuck. It was the voice from those weird calls earlier. She gasped and rolled over, then scooted right to the far edge of the bed. She stared across the room. The woman from outside stood by the door with her hands behind her back, and in the darkness, she looked like a slim black bowling pin with a face and hair on top. Her skin was white, so white, just like it had been outside, and her lips were dark.

The woman flicked the light on. Felicity blinked at the harshness and stared at her, heart thumping, her pulse throbbing hard in her neck.

Christ, the woman's cheeks were rubbery. Was that…was that a *mask*?

"Get the hell out," Felicity managed, her chest hurting, sharp pains shooting across it. She reached for her phone, but it was too far away now. The nightstand on the other side of the bed might as well be a mile in the distance for all the good it did her.

"I don't think so. My name's Bête Noir, by the way. You can just call me Bête. It means so many things. Bad news, enemy, devil..." Bête moved closer, bringing her hands around the front.

A knife blade glinted in one fist.

Jesus Christ, no...

"What...what do you want?" Felicity asked, eyeing the door and gauging whether she could leg it past her and find help. She couldn't just stay here and be a willing victim.

I'm not going to make it. She'll stab me as soon as I get close.

"I want the truth to come out," Bête said. "For my story to be heard. I tried to speak to you last week, but you weren't interested."

Felicity couldn't for the life of her work out who Bête could be. "Who...who are you?"

Bête gestured to her mask. "Doesn't this give you a clue?"

What was she on about? Why would a mask mean anything?

Blinking, the cogs turning but nothing coming up to help her, Felicity frowned. "Please, I have money. Take my money. My TV. Anything."

"I don't want your fucking money or your bloody TV."

God, that voice. It was like someone talking while being strangled — raspy, breathy, broken. A shiver tickled up Felicity's spine, and she fought a shudder. She didn't want this woman to know she was afraid. Calling on her Talk Today training, Felicity opted for the calm and level-headed approach. It always worked on the callers.

"If you'd like help, I can do that. If you need someone to talk to, I can do that, too," she said. It had to work. It was all she had to give.

"Talk?" Bête snorted. "Like I just said, I tried, and you weren't interested. In Vicky's Café. You were drinking a coffee. Eating a Danish. Reading your Kindle. Remember that day, do you? Is it coming back to you now?"

Felicity couldn't get a handle on this. Was Bête *him*? "Why are you...dressed like that?"

"Why not?"

"And talking like that?"

"Why. The. Fuck. Not?" Bête came closer, the knife tip an arm's length away. Too close. Too scary. "Flat on your back. Now. If you don't..."

Felicity did as she'd been told. She'd play along. Talk to him. Get him to see sense. She'd been through worse than this and got out alive. "Why are you doing this?"

"Like you don't know." Bête slid the knife into a sheath on his belt then pulled some rope from the big pocket on the front of the hoodie.

"No…I have no idea. Come on. There's no need for that. I don't even know why you're doing this, I swear." Was he part of *their* gang? Had he approached her in the café because they'd told him to reel her back in? Take her back *there*?

If her legs would carry her to the door, she'd give them a try, but they'd gone to jelly. Her skin went cold, and sweat coated her, bringing on a chill. Or was that fear? "Look, let's talk about this. Please?"

She sounded whiny and detested herself for it.

Bête stared down at her, that mask so fucking freaky, his breaths loud behind it. Wheezy. Wind through a gap in the window. "It's too late."

"But why?" She hated how it had come out as a wail. A kid trying to get their own way.

Bête climbed on the bed and straddled her, then dropped the rope beside them. Felicity's fight or flight response kicked in, and she bucked, raising her hands to claw at the mask. Bête growled and grabbed a strand of rope and, despite Felicity's attempts at fighting him off, her wrist was secured to the bedpost. She parted her lips to scream, but he anticipated her and

12

quickly withdrew a rag from his pocket, stuffing it in her mouth. The material had her gagging. It smelled and tasted of dirty washing. She had to breathe through her nose and couldn't get enough air in, panic urging her to suck in more oxygen, whispering that she was going to die if she didn't.

With her other wrist tied up at the opposite corner, he got off her and swept away her legs as she kicked out, easily managing to rope her ankles to the bottom posts as if she wasn't fighting at all. Her muscles protested at being stretched so much, and her armpits ached from the pressure.

"Now," Bête said. "I'm going to make you sorry."

Sorry for what? She tried to say that, but it was a garbled, muffled mess.

"I'll tell you, shall I?" Bête asked.

Felicity nodded, frantic, ready to do anything he wanted so he'd go away and leave her alone. Because he would. He'd done it before. He'd followed her around, turning up wherever she was. She'd asked him not to after the night club incident, and he'd gone.

For a while.

Until she'd seen him in the café.

Bête walked to the side of the bed and leant over, the nose of the mask almost touching hers. It smelled so horrible.

"I'm going to kill you because you said no," he whispered.

Then he used the knife to slice open her pyjama top and bent down to sniff her nipples.

Oh God, Oh God, please, not that…

But he didn't do that.

Instead, he plunged the knife deep and said, "One…"

Felicity weaved around on the dance floor, her mind fuddled with alcohol, her tongue furry from it. Becky had gone off somewhere with a bloke, probably for a good old snog in the corner. She'd better be back soon, otherwise Felicity would be going home without her. Staying here in this state wasn't a good move. She'd drunk far too much, and her body and mind didn't seem like it belonged to her anymore.

She bumped into a woman gyrating in the extreme and rebounded off her, backing into another person. Spinning round, she gazed at him. He was the same height as her, but stockier, and that must be why she hadn't knocked him flying. She reckoned he weighed about sixteen stone. His muscles had muscles.

"Sorry," she said, the word slurred, elongated, and showing her up for the drunkard she was. "I just…" She hiccupped. "I've had one too many."

"I can see that," he said, frowning. "Let me take you home."

She waved off that suggestion. Gone were the days she accepted a man going back to her place. There was no way she'd do that now, and she didn't go out enough to meet many people, preferring not to engage in conversation much anymore, except with Becky. Since she'd been nabbed off the street and driven to a house where men had pawed her, expected things of her she'd hadn't thought she'd have to give, she'd vowed never to trust a bloke again unless he could prove he was one hundred percent genuine. Especially not a stranger, although this man seemed familiar. She couldn't for the life of her place where she'd seen him before, though.

Is he one of them?

In case he wasn't, she decided to play nice. "No. Thanks anyway, but I'm here with my friend." *She glanced about, aware of him studying her, staring so hard it seemed to burn her skin. But that was only her cheeks flushing — not from embarrassment but from being damn uncomfortable. And a speck of fear, she'd acknowledge that. He was a tad creepy, standing stock still like that, arms down by his sides, fists clenched as if he was ready to punch her lights out.*

"I'll sort you a taxi then," *he said, pushing the issue. He was obviously the sort who didn't like being told no.* "And I'll wait outside with you until it arrives." *An order, not a suggestion.*

"No," *she snapped, a bit too harshly, but God, why couldn't he just take no for an answer?* "It's fine. I'm going to…"

She didn't finish, just staggered off, pushing through the throng of manic dancers, Eminem giving it his all, rapping his heart out, God bless the dishy bastard. She sought Becky out. Thank Christ, there she was, standing by the bar, chortling at something or other a blond man said. Felicity wished she could get on with men so easily, but the past had ruined that.

Felicity stumbled over to her, and Becky turned, eyes wide.

"Oh shit. Time to go home," Becky said. "What the bloody hell have you drunk?"

That was the thing. Felicity recalled guzzling only three bottles of Smirnoff Ice, so there was no way she should be this pissed. She held up the right amount of fingers and stared at them, seeing six instead of three.

"What's up with you then?" Becky asked, guiding her towards the door. "Didn't you have any dinner before we came out? Drinking on an empty stomach isn't good, love. And you need to be careful. People put shit in your drinks these days."

Felicity nodded, past caring now. She just wanted to go home.

As they neared the door, the man from the dance floor stepped forward and, when Felicity passed him, he whispered in her ear, "You made a big mistake."

Shivers crept through her, and she darted outside, almost turning her ankle she was that desperate to get away from him.

The inside of a taxi had never felt so good.

Home was even better.

For weeks after that night, she kept seeing him. In the street, in shops, in Vicky's Café. In her damn street.

In her bed. Over her. Plunging a knife into her stomach and saying, "Two… Three… Four…"

Then she didn't see him at all. There was nothing, a blank void, and she sank into it, welcoming the blessed relief that it was over. All of it. Her past, present, and future.

CHAPTER TWO

Helena cracked up laughing. She'd been to the gym with Andy earlier and kept remembering him falling backwards off the treadmill and landing on his arse in front of a few seasoned gym-goers using the ellipticals. He was currently rubbing his tailbone while she sat in her office chair opposite, doodling on a pad. Him coming in was a welcome break from the mountain of paperwork she needed to check for the Walker case. She hadn't thought she'd ever say seeing him would be a good thing, but since they'd been making an effort to get along, he didn't seem so bad now.

"Stop it," he said, sitting on the spare seat in front of her desk.

"Come on now. It *was* funny, though."

"For you maybe. I'm not going to be able to face those blokes in there again. Did you see the way one of them trainer fellas tried not to laugh, the git?"

Helena smiled. "You're not giving up. We need to get you fit." He needn't think a little tumble would get him off the hook.

"Hmm." He rubbed his chin. "Slave driver."

Her desk phone rang, cutting her off mid-chuckle. "Helena Stratton."

"Hi, guv. Louise here."

Helena imagined Louise leaning on the front desk, one leg bent at the knee, twirling her foot. "What's up?"

"You're needed. A Felicity Greaves has been found dead at her home."

"Oh, poor thing." At the same time, she thought uncharitably: *Wonderful. Just what we need, another body straight after the Walkers have been bumped off.* "Address, please."

"Seventeen Kew Road."

"Right. How old is she?" Not that it mattered. A body was a body as far as she was concerned, and she'd treat the case just as importantly as any other, even though she'd have preferred a bit of a break in between.

Pack it in, thinking like that.

"Thirty-one," Louise said. "Lives alone. SOCO are already there because Clive called it in."

"Okay. I'll ring Zach. Me and Andy are on our way. Thanks." She put the phone down and gave her partner a wan smile.

"No rest for the wicked?" he asked.

"Nope." She briefed him quickly, then rang Zach. "Hi. Can't talk." *Please get the hint that I'm with someone...* "I have an address for you. A deceased female."

"Bloody hell," Zach said. "I take it you have company?"

"Yes."

"So I can't tell you how much I'm looking forward to tonight?"

"No." If Andy wasn't there, she'd squirm. But he was, so she didn't.

"Shame. Catch you in a bit."

She docked the phone and looked at Andy. "Come on, you. Just as well we didn't go for an early lunch, isn't it. God knows what's in store for us. I wouldn't want you puking at a scene."

"Since when have I puked?"

She dug her elbow into his ribs and winked. They walked into the incident room. Olivia and Phil were at their desks, backs to the room.

"Guys, sorry, but we've got another case," Helena said. "Shame it's literally days after the Walkers, but killers don't tend to be considerate, do they. You two can sort it between you as to who's doing what. A Felicity Greaves, thirty-one, seventeen Kew Road. All I know is she's

21

dead — I'm assuming it's murder or suspicious, otherwise we wouldn't be on it. Find the next of kin if there is one. Do the usual digging. See you later."

She left with Andy and drove them to Kew Road, up the cliff close to where Emma Walker had lived, just a few streets away. Police cars were parked outside Felicity's opposite, as well as a SOCO van. Clive, a uniform, stood at the gate, and two others were talking at front doors. Several onlookers stared from their windows, most of them elderly, their white-haired heads giving their age away.

Helena and Andy crossed the road.

"All right, guv," Clive said, holding out the scene log.

She signed it. "Not too bad." She handed the log to Andy and peered over Clive's shoulder at the property behind him. A bungalow. "You?"

"A bit shaken, to be honest." Clive shrugged. "But I'm sure I'll get over it."

"Were you the first on scene?" Helena nosed through the gap where the front door stood ajar. A hallway with an open door at the end.

"Yes. I got asked to call round because she hadn't turned up for work, which is unusual. Her colleague, who is also her friend, said the deceased was frightened of some men or other coming to find her, so she wanted us to see if Miss Greaves was all right. Something to do with...um..." He seemed to find the ground interesting. "Uthway."

Helena's guts rolled. That man would be the death of her. All her colleagues knew what had happened to her, hence Clive grimacing at having to bring the man's name up again.

"What? Had she been held by him for trafficking then?" she asked.

"From what I could gather, yes. Her friend did a lot of babbling, but I got the gist that Miss Greaves didn't tell her about any of it until she'd got away from them. I've got her mate's name and address here. You might get more sense out of her than I did. She was in a right old state, if you ask me." He pulled out his notebook.

Andy did the same and jotted down the info as Clive read it out.

"Fab. We'll go and see her in a few." Helena licked her suddenly dry lips and tasted salt from the sea air. "So you went inside because? I mean, you've covered your arse, right? Had probable cause?"

Clive nodded. "One of the neighbours reported a woman hanging about last night, just after eleven. I opened the letterbox and...the smell of blood was a bit ripe."

"Okay. Nice." She waved and made her way up the path, slipping on booties and gloves outside the door. She stepped into the hall, and immediately, the scent of hot pennies smacked

23

into her. Breathing through her mouth, she walked farther in then poked her head around a doorframe.

SOCOs milled about in a living room. It was clean, tidy, with no sign of a disturbance. Felicity clearly liked things orderly. The scatter cushions on the sofa were placed so they resembled diamond shapes.

"Where's the victim, please?" she asked one of them.

"Next room along, guv," he said, his voice muffled by the mask. "Tom's in there."

She smiled. Her favourite SOCO.

Andy trailed her down the hall, and Helena stared through the open doorway. A brunette woman, bound to the double bed posts with rope, had her pyjamas sliced off, the pink remnants either side of her. The sheets had once been a pristine white, but blood had soon fucked that up. Her quilt was bunched in places beneath her, as though she'd been under it at some point, then had got up.

A photographer took a few more shots, and Helena glanced at where the lens pointed.

Blood on the walls. So much of it. Arcs, splashes from castoff, yet there wasn't a lot on the ceiling, just on a rectangular patch. What was that all about? Movement to her right caught her attention. Tom was bent over, rooting around in a chest of drawers.

"Hi," she said.

He turned his head, straightened, and used his white suit cuff to move his face mask down. "That," he said, pointing at the walls, "is the result of one angry person. She was stabbed multiple times, as you can see from her stomach."

Helena had chosen not to focus on that, even though she knew what was there—a mess of tangled innards on display.

"See how the spatter just stops inside lines on the walls and ceiling?" he asked.

She nodded. "Whoever it was had been in a frenzy." She nodded at the blood patterns on the wall. "Handprint."

"Gloves, unfortunately. Seems they maybe needed to steady themselves at one point," Tom said. "Oddly, not much blood on the floor."

Helena stared at it. Just a few droplets on the laminate closest to the bed. "How is that possible with such a manic attack?"

"No idea, but the evidence doesn't lie." Tom shrugged.

"Hello?" Zach called.

Helena faced the hallway where she'd come in. Zach walked towards them, just visible behind Andy, who moved to one side to let the medical examiner past. Zach stood beside her in the doorway and took in the room, his forehead scrunched.

"Christ," he said. "All right to come in, Tom?"

Tom nodded. Helena and Zach scooted along, and the photographer left, going into the living room. Zach walked to the bed and stood beside it. Helena glanced away while he took her rectal temperature, and Andy pulled a face. He wasn't enjoying this. Neither was she, but it was their job, so they'd have to suck it up.

A minute or so passed.

"Estimated time of death, close to midnight," Zach said.

Helena returned her attention to the room. Zach leant over the bed, peering at Felicity's open stomach. Tom cleared his throat.

"Diary, guv," he said, holding up a pink book with a suede-like cover. He handed it to her.

Helena flicked through to the most recent entry.

I had a nightmare again. About them. They're coming for me, I know it, but I can't talk to anyone except Becky. Who else would believe me, anyway, after all the lies I used to tell? The girl who cried wolf, that's what they'd say, but it's true, what happened. It really is.

I think about it all the time. Those other girls. The young men. How we were squashed into that room together, basically sleeping like dogs, layers of people waiting to be sold. Waiting to escape. Wanting to die.

It's only a matter of time before they come back and continue what they started. Before they look for me. I know things — and they know I do. I can get them right in the shit. Eventually, he'll turn up and shut my mouth for good.

If Felicity had been talking about Uthway, Helena could well believe he'd come back, too. She also had nightmares. How many others did? How many people suffered night after night, dreading that knock on the door?

Or someone breaking in and doing...this?

Was this Uthway? Would Helena be next?

She closed the book, giving it back to Tom to put in an evidence bag. "I need that back at the station as soon as possible so Ol or Phil can have a look at it, see if there's something we can use."

Tom nodded. "He got in through the back door, by the way. In the kitchen. There's a dog in there, crated. Poor thing's scared shitless. I've called the local rescue home to collect him for now until we know if she has any family who might be willing to take him on."

"I'd say Felicity was on her own. Ol would have rung by now if she'd found any relatives." Helena sighed. "Listen, we're going to shoot off to speak to the neighbour who saw the woman hanging around last night, then we need to see Felicity's friend."

"Right," Zach said. "This is going to take me a while, so other than her being stabbed, I don't have anything much to give you yet."

"Right-handed," Tom said. "You can tell by where the blood is on the wall. We'll get the spatter studied and should be able to tell you how tall the killer is likely to be, going by the height of the arcs and whatnot."

"Thanks," she said. "I'd say have a nice day, but…"

She lifted a hand in a half-arsed wave and followed Andy into the kitchen. The dog whimpered, cowering in the corner of the metal crate. Helena had the urge to pet it, to calm it, but Andy called her over to the back door.

"The key's in the lock, glass smashed." He stared at her, probably waiting for an answer.

"Right. I wonder if Felicity heard it being broken — or anyone else for that matter."

"Might have used a cloth over the hand — less noise."

"Hmm."

She led the way out into the front garden. They removed their booties and gloves, disposing of them in a black bag beside the door. At the gate, she asked Clive who the witness neighbour was.

"Over the road there, look." He pointed at an old granny nosing through her window. "She's a bit shaky, as you can imagine. A Mrs Jean Salter, seventy-four."

"Okie dokie." Helena crossed the road and went up the woman's path. She held her ID up at the window, and the lady vanished, reappearing as a silhouette behind the opaque door glass.

"Come in," Mrs Salter said. "I have a pot of tea in the living room. Would you like one?"

"Ooh, yes please." Helena smiled.

Andy nodded as an answer and shut the door. Mrs Salter trotted along the hallway into the kitchen. She returned carrying two cups and went into the living room. Helena and Andy sat on an armchair each, while Mrs Salter lowered to the sofa and poured the drinks through a strainer.

"Help yourself to milk and sugar," she said, gesturing to the tray on the coffee table.

Once they'd all got settled, Helena smiled then took a sip. Why was tea from a pot so much better? It reminded her of going to her nan's as a kid.

"This is lovely, Mrs Salter," she said.

"Oh, it's Jean. Call me Jean." She beamed, showing a set of dentures.

"Can you tell me what you saw last night?"

Jean, a spindly little thing, with twig-like arms and a puff of lilac hair, cradled her flower-painted cup and stared out of the window. "I couldn't sleep—damn wind was a bit noisy last night, wasn't it. We never did get the full brunt of that hurricane yet, did we. I expect it'll be here over the next day or so." She gazed into thin air then seemed to remember she'd been asked a question. "Anyway, I got out of bed and made a drink—hot milk, sugar, a squirt of honey—and had a nose outside. It's calming to do that, don't you think, when the rest of the world is asleep or close to it, and the street becomes just a silent strip of homes, no kids messing about or people being noisy." She turned and gazed at Helena with rheumy eyes.

"Yes, there's too much noise about these days." Helena nodded.

"Isn't there just. Well, there was a lady in the street, and she was standing right there, on the other side of my fence."

Helena stood and peered outside, then sat again. "Go on."

"She had one of those tops on, you know the ones all the young folks wear, with a hood. It was black, same as her jeans and shoes, but I didn't see those until she crossed the road. She was a bit...beefy for a woman. She had long blonde hair, and it was like she knew I was watching. She turned to peer inside here, and I was glad I hadn't put the light on, I can tell you. She would have seen me staring, wouldn't she. But I got a good look at her—the streetlamp shone on her, see. Delicate features. Dark lipstick, though. It seemed black to me, but it could have been red." She bit her lip. "I don't know."

"What happened then?" Helena asked.

"She walked over the road to that bungalow there, where Felicity lives, and tried pulling the handle down on the front door."

Helena jolted at that and glanced at Andy. He raised his eyebrows. Maybe whoever it was had decided going in through the front was too risky.

"Those bungalows have lovely views from the back," Jean went on. "Nothing else behind them except the cliff top, then the sea for miles and miles."

"How would a person get into the rear garden, do you know?" Helena asked.

"Oh, there's an alleyway next to number twenty. Me and Gladys—that's Felicity's gran, God rest her soul—used to nip down there in the summer to have a bit of a sunbathe. Lots of people do it. Saves going down to the beach."

"Does Felicity have any other family?"

Jean shook her head. "No. All alone now, she is." She sipped some tea. "Got to love PG Tips. What's happened over there? I hope Felicity is all right."

Helena wasn't sure whether to tell the woman anything or not. "Do you know her well?"

"Of course! I've known her since she was born. Me and Gladys have lived here since these were built. Council, you know, except we bought them years down the line. Gladys left hers to Felicity."

"I see. What about Felicity's parents?"

"They're dead. The mother was always a rum sort, gave poor Gladys hell, and she threw herself off the cliff when Felicity's dad had an accident in his lorry. Killed him, it did."

Tragic. "How old was Felicity when this happened?"

"Two. So she's never remembered them." Jean wiped at her eye. "Still, she's a good girl, never a moment's trouble from her. She gets my shopping, you know, and she's one of them Talk Today people."

Andy scribbled that down.

"Where did she work?" Helena drank some tea. Yes, you did have to love a bit of PG.

"In the arcade. The poor thing couldn't get a job anywhere else once she was made redundant at the biscuit factory. Still, it's just something to tide her over, and Gladys left her a fair few bob, so she'll be all right for the time being."

"Do you know whether she was having any trouble from anyone?"

"Who, Felicity?" Jean tittered. "No, she's a dear soul. Wouldn't hurt a fly."

Helena resisted closing her eyes and muttering, "Typical!"

"I'll pop over to see her later, once all the police have gone." Jean popped her cup on the

32

table. "Why are you here? Did that woman do something?"

Helena stood, and Andy followed suit.

"I'll send someone over to give you the details," Helena said. *What a coward I am.* "Thank you for your time. You've been very helpful."

Helena escaped, rushing out and across the road. She told Clive to ask one of the door-to-door officers to speak to Jean, then she got in the car. Andy joined her, and they drove in silence to see Becky Jermaine, Felicity's friend.

Let's see what she has to say, shall we?

CHAPTER THREE

He stood in front of a fruit machine in Smaltern Amusements, beside the red money exchange booth. The old bat in there was talking to a customer through the semicircle cut-out of the plastic partition, bending over so her words carried. She ought to keep her voice down really, but she'd always been a strident bitch, her tone loud. Still, she was doing him a favour by being so gobby, so he wasn't complaining.

He remembered her from his childhood, when she'd had long brown hair instead of the grey effort that seemed to hover over her head as though it wasn't even attached. She'd had one of those perms, he reckoned, as if it was something every woman did when they hit sixty. Like it was the law they had to have gran hair. Once smooth skin had given way to deep crevices that mapped out how hard her life had been. Go down that line, it signified her bastard of a husband, go down another, and it led to the story of how her kids had wreaked havoc. All the others were sentences and paragraphs of a sorry tale she enjoyed telling to anyone who'd listen.

"No," Mouth Almighty said. "Didn't turn up for work, did she, so Becky went off on one, panicking, although why she did that is anyone's guess."

"Think it's anything serious?" the customer asked, a bloke of about fifty, his paunch the size of a full bag of shopping, the hair at his temples a fuzzy grey.

"Well, Becky seemed to think so. She darted off after she rang Felicity, who didn't answer, by the way. These young girls, all so dramatic, aren't they?" She pursed her lips. "Anyway, Becky ended up going home—too upset, she said—so we're two people short. I'm just waiting for that lad Glen to turn up. He's a good kid. Never lets me down. A bit dopey, though."

The man nodded, sage as you like, sucking in his bottom lip. "I could work here, you know. I wouldn't let you down either. Early retirement isn't all I thought it would be. I'm bored, to be honest."

"Now there's a thought." She rubbed her bristly chin. "I could do with someone like you. Reliable and all that."

While they prattled on, he slid the last pound into the slot machine and pressed the various flashing buttons. Three lemons came up, and he banked the winnings. Then three bars, and he'd made back the money he'd laid out. Coins chugged out into the tray, and he scooped them up.

"'Ere," Mouth Almighty said. "I'll have to ban you if you keep winning." She cackled, as though what she'd said was well funny.

It wasn't.

He resisted giving her the middle finger and walked out, blinking at the brightness of the day compared to the almost seedy shadows of the arcade. Gulls squawked, zooming at him from on high, the dumb bastards probably thinking he had a bag of chips on him that they could nick.

"Fuck off," he said, walking along the street then entering the little shop he'd loved as a kid, the one that sold sticks of rock, postcards, and stupid ornaments with Smaltern written on plaques at the bases. Who the hell bought that sort of shit?

He swiped up a magazine and a Mars bar, then popped them on the counter. Den, the old bloke who owned the place, pointed the barcode scanner at the items. He was surprised the elderly git had moved with the times and got rid of his old-fashioned till.

"Two pounds and tuppence," Den said, giving him a filthy look.

The bastard always had stared at him that way, and he was getting sick of it.

He paid, all but throwing the coins at him, then grabbed up his stuff and left the shop. Down the alley between Den's and an ice cream shop, he paused, scoffing his Mars while checking whether anyone was going to appear. They didn't, so he walked round the back of Den's and stared at the flat above, then at the door. It wasn't anything special, nothing that could keep him out, and it wasn't like he hadn't checked it before now. Fuck, he'd spent years plotting all this, so he knew it would be easy to break in. Den didn't have an alarm. He was old-school in that regard and still believed no one would rob him, the twat.

The lack of one would be his downfall.

CHAPTER FOUR

Helena knocked on Becky Jermaine's door, and it swung open a few seconds later. Holding up her ID, Helena introduced herself and Andy.

"Oh God, come in," Becky said, white as anything, her makeup streaked around the eyes as though she'd been crying. Her blonde hair was sleek and straight, hanging well past her shoulders.

Helena and Andy stepped inside, and Becky led them to the kitchen—pine cabinets, yellow walls, and a white blind with a row of daisies along the bottom. A load of washing swished around in the machine, bubbles pressing against the glass door along with what appeared to be a black sock asking to be let out.

"Would you like a cuppa?" Becky reached for the sunshine-coloured kettle, her nails painted red.

Callie Walker popped into Helena's head, and she shoved the image away.

"No, thank you." Helena smiled. "We've just had one. Unless you want another, Andy?" She turned to look at him.

He shook his head. "Not for me. Cheers for the offer, though."

Bloody hell, he's mellowing.

"Right. Well…" Becky stood by the sink, twiddling her thumbs, a diamond ring glinting on her finger. Engaged but not married?

"Let's have a sit down, shall we?" Helena gestured to the pine table and chairs.

Once they were all seated, she smiled again at Becky and asked, "When you spoke to an officer earlier, you indicated a man or men were coming for Felicity. Can you elaborate on that, please?"

Becky took a deep breath. "I probably didn't make much sense when I spoke to him. I was that frightened when she didn't turn up for work or answer her phone. The policeman nipped in to see me at work before he went to Felicity's, and then I came home. Couldn't face it with the worry, you know. But yes, after Felicity got away from them, she told me all about it but wouldn't go to the police. She reckoned if she did, they'd find out."

"Okay. Do you know who 'they' are?" Uthway's face loomed in Helena's mind, and she shuddered. What was with the images bugging her today?

"Not names, no, but they were running some sort of trafficking ring, so she said." Becky laced her fingers on the table. "It was in the news a few months later, and Felicity kept crying about it all."

So did I.

"Can I ask why *you* didn't tell the police?" Helena raised her eyebrows. She shouldn't be so hard on her, giving that sort of look, but it was done now.

Becky squirmed. "Felicity begged me not to, and I know it was wrong, but I didn't want to let her down. And…" She bit her lip. "God, this is going to sound awful, but Felicity told a lot of lies, so I kind of…" She covered her face with her hands and moaned.

"You didn't quite believe her?" Helena supplied.

Becky drew her hands down, revealing a blush. "Sorry to say it, but no, I didn't, not until it came on telly. If I'd been held captive, you can bet I'd have gone to the police first. As soon as I got out of that house, that's what I'd have done.

41

You wouldn't see me just going home and trying to forget about it."

People assumed all the time. They couldn't possibly understand someone else's experience if they hadn't been through it themselves. They could empathise and imagine, but that was about it.

"Not everyone thinks straight in those sorts of situations," Helena said gently. "We all process things differently, and we think about what we'd do, but when the reality of it is right in front of you, many people do the opposite of what they thought they would." She knew that. She'd sat in that grimy corner in the storage container and had given up the fight, too scared to do much else. Her training had deserted her after she'd been abused, not to mention the fact they'd injected her with something that had sent her groggy.

"Oh, I didn't mean... I just thought..." A tear slipped down Becky's cheek, and she swiped it away with the back of her hand. "This isn't coming out right. Let me start again. I believed her but at the same time I didn't. She hasn't ever made anything up like *that* before, so part of me wanted to support her, I still do. I was worried that by me going to the police it might make things worse. You know, they'd really come back. Is that what's happened? Have they taken her away again?"

"No, they haven't taken her away." Helena swallowed. "Where did she say she was when they had her?"

"Some house in Lime Street." She clapped a hand over her mouth. "Shit."

Helena shook her head. "No need to fret. They're not there anymore." Lime Street was where Helena had been spying on them and that fucking great hulk of a bloke had dragged her away to the storage container. "None of them are around at the moment, so nothing to worry about there." *I bloody hope.* "However, someone did pay Felicity a visit last night, so I'd like to know whether there's anyone else you can think of who would be 'after' her."

"Someone else?" Becky squeaked. "Is she all right?"

"Try to think," Helena evaded. "If she told a lot of lies in the past, maybe someone is upset with her and they've been holding a grudge. What sort of lies were they?"

Becky flapped her hand in front of her face as if those lies loomed in front of her and she wanted to bat them away. "Oh, just stupid things. Like she had a boyfriend when she didn't—she was fifteen at the time, so looking back on it, I'm putting it down to her just being a young girl who wanted to fit in with everyone else. She lied about her exam results, said she was moving abroad, all sorts of things really.

There was always a white one somewhere, but she's nice, so I didn't pull her up on it. I felt sorry for her, being brought up by her gran and not having a mum and dad."

"So would that have upset anyone, the white lies?"

"Not that I can see. I mean, we all fib at some point, don't we? They didn't do any harm. So no, I don't think anyone else apart from those men would come for her."

"It's a pretty serious situation we have here, and I want you to think carefully. Do you know of a woman who would want to harm Felicity?"

Becky's mouth sagged open. "What? No! She rarely talks to anyone we knew as kids. She's just got me now, oh, and Jean over the road. Since she escaped from Lime Street, she's been pretty vacant. You know, seems lost inside her head. She jumps at everything. Then when the Walkers got murdered... She convinced herself they'd been killed for escaping as well. Once it came out it was someone else who'd done it, she calmed down."

Helena could cry. That poor woman must have been a nervous wreck. Helena had had counselling, and she'd barely managed to cope at first, so God knew what Felicity had been going through with only one friend to tell.

"Do you have anyone who can come and sit with you for a bit?" Helena asked. Shit, it was time for breaking the news, and she didn't want to leave Becky alone afterwards.

"What for?" Becky frowned and cocked her head.

"Do you?"

"My mum lives next door to the left. Let me just go and get her." She made to rise.

"No, no. Andy will do that." Helena smiled.

Andy left the house. Becky settled back down and stared behind Helena.

"Something horrible has happened, hasn't it," Becky said.

"I'm afraid so." Helena took a deep breath. "I'm so sorry to have to tell you, but Felicity was murdered last night."

"What?" It came out as a screech. Becky shot up out of her chair and slapped her palms on the table, leaning on them. "What...what happened?" She went white again, and tears welled up. Her eyes held a frightened glint, as though she had the urge to run out of there, as if that would make this all go away.

But you can't run from your troubles. They live in your head.

"Please, have a seat again." Helena blew out a breath while the woman sat. "It's all very upsetting, I know. Someone broke in and killed her. I won't give you the details, but we need to find who did this as quickly as possible. Are you *sure* you don't know of any woman who might have wanted to do this?"

Becky wiped her face. "A *woman*?"

While Becky hadn't broken down yet, Helena guessed the shock would set in soon, so she'd grab the chance to press her a little more, cruel as that may seem.

"It could be something as slight as a small argument," she said.

Becky shook her head. "Seriously? A tiff from years ago could result in…in *this*? Who the fuck goes around killing people because they've been upset?"

"I'm afraid some people carry things inside them for years, and this sort of occurrence is the result. It isn't logical, I realise that. You can't imagine someone doing this because *you* wouldn't do it, but there are those who think this is acceptable behaviour."

"How can murder be acceptable?" Becky shook her head, like it would shuffle all her no doubt racing thoughts into some sort of order so they made sense.

"Do you remember anything that could help us?" Helena asked softly.

"No. My head's so full. I can't think…"

Helena understood that. She'd felt the same on many occasions. She was about to offer some comfort, but Andy came back in with a woman of about sixty. Upon seeing her, Becky blarted, and the lady rushed to her daughter, gathering her into her arms.

Helena moved close to Andy and whispered, "Did you tell the mum?"

He nodded.

They stood there for a while, heads bent, Helena feeling all kinds of awkward, then Becky stopped sobbing and looked their way, blinking, zoned out.

"If you think of anything..." Helena reached into her pocket for a card and handed it over to the mother — Becky was in no fit state to take it. "Ring me. We'll leave you be for now, and once again, I'm sorry to have brought you this news. Thank you for your help."

They left the house, and in the car, Helena shook. Talking about Uthway and his men had left a sour taste in her mouth. She remembered the smell of his breath, his body odour, and how he'd touched her in places he had no right to, 'road testing' her body to see if she was good enough to be sold.

Andy got in and rummaged in the glove box for a sweet. He gave it to her.

"Thanks," she said, unwrapping it. She did like a Werther's.

"The taste will give you something else to think about," he said.

Fuck. Why had she ever thought he was a know-it-all dickhead who only had himself in mind?

She blinked, started the car, and sucked on the sweet. Driving off, she pushed all the thoughts out of her head that wanted to crowd it, and headed for the station. She needed to brief Ol and Phil on everything, plus get any info off them. So far, though, it was looking likely that once again they didn't have much to go on. Just the lady in the street and another who told too many lies and had ended up dead, possibly for that very reason.

The sight of Felicity in her bed flashed in front of her, and she almost swerved into the kerb. "Fuck me!"

"You all right?" Andy asked.

"Yeah." Was it only a short while ago she'd laughed her arse off at him landing on his backside at the gym? It was times like these when she thought she'd never find anything funny ever again. Who the hell had wanted Felicity dead? What on earth had she done to anger someone so much? And why was the blood scant on the floor?

"It's already doing your head in, isn't it?" Andy asked.

"How can you tell?" She pulled into the station car park.

"Because you're crunching on that bloody sweet like a maniac."

She swallowed the bits and cut the engine. "Sorry if the noise was annoying. Didn't realise I was doing it." She hated loud eaters, and she'd just become one.

"Not a problem."

They entered the station, and Louise waved them over to the front desk.

"Tom rang and asked me to pass on the message that the diary is with Olivia and Phil." Louise jerked her head, beckoning them closer. "And I had a weird phone call."

"Oh right. How so?" Helena asked.

"They said they'd normally ring Talk Today, but 'seeing as the bitch I usually talk to is dead, you'll have to do.' That's what they said. I thought that a bit odd, to be honest."

"I don't," Helena said. "Felicity Greaves worked for Talk Today. We'll be nipping there once we've had a team chat. What did they want?"

"Oh, they said they wanted to make friends. I said I wasn't in the habit of doing that with strangers on the other end of the phone, and they asked if I'd like to have a coffee so we weren't strangers anymore. I said no. That was it."

"Thanks for letting me know. Phone number from whoever rang?"

"Yep, and it's a pay-as-you-go. I gave Olivia the info, and she said she'd look into it."

"Right, thanks." Helena sighed. "We'll be off then."

Upstairs, she walked into the incident room and stood by the large whiteboard. Andy slumped onto his desk chair, spreading his legs out in front of him and linking his hands over his belly. Ol and Phil twisted in their seats to face her.

Helena told them about the crime scene, their visit with Jean Salter, and also with Becky Jermaine. "It's all a bit crap really. We have a woman who could have done this — well, I'm sure we do. She wouldn't be trying the front door handle to get in otherwise, would she?"

"Unless she was a friend nipping round," Phil suggested.

"At that time of night, though? Becky said Felicity didn't have any mates bar her, not these days. It seems Felicity withdrew into herself since supposedly being in Lime Street." Christ, it sounded as if Helena didn't believe the Uthway tale either, but with no proof Felicity was ever in that house or anywhere near Uthway and his men, she couldn't treat it as fact, just supposition. "Okay, what about that phone call Louise got. Anything on that, Ol?"

"Yes, but nothing that will help us. It was sent from the manufacturer to Phone City in town and paid for with cash last week — I rang them to check. They have no cameras inside the shop, and Phil contacted CCTV, and the cameras in the side street where Phone City is aren't bloody working at the moment. Haven't been for a fortnight."

"For fuck's sake." Helena sighed. "Is it me, or does this kind of thing always happen to us? It's like the universe conspires against us every time we get a case."

Ol smiled sadly, and Phil scratched his head. Andy added a grunt and rubbed his belly for good measure.

"What about the diary?"

"Nothing we can use," Phil said. "I'm only halfway through it, but it just goes on about 'them', whoever they are."

"Well, plod on. We're going to the Talk Today office. Where the hell is that, d'you know?" Helena turned to put info on the whiteboard. The marker pen squeaked with every letter she wrote.

Someone clacked on a keyboard behind her.

"Above Chargrill Kebabs," Phil said. "The high street."

"Okay, thanks." She scribbled a few more notes, annoyed with herself for not asking Becky if she had a recent photo of Felicity so they could pin it up to remind them who they were fighting for. "Ol, can you get a phone number for Becky

Jermaine and give her a ring for me. Ask her to send you a picture of Felicity if she has one. Print it out and stick it up here." She tapped the board.

"Okay, guv."

Helena put the marker down and faced them all. "Then do your usual checks while me and Andy go into town."

She gestured to him with her head, and he hauled himself from his seat and followed her to the car. The journey to town didn't take long, and she managed to nab a parking space right in front of the kebab place. She got out, and a traffic warden was writing a ticket for someone a few cars up. Hoping for the best, Helena approached him, showed her badge, and explained their need to park for a few minutes. She expected him to be a jobsworth and tell her to pay anyway, but he wrote in a notebook and signed the bottom of the page, then ripped it off and handed it to her.

"Just pop that on the dash," he said. "I'm off elsewhere in a minute, but that'll do just in case another warden comes by before you leave. They shouldn't, because this is *my* patch, but you never know."

"Thanks," she said. "You're a star."

He beamed at that, the skin beside his eyes crinkling, and she left him to get on. Outside Chargrill, she was about to go inside when

Andy pointed at a second door, grey with a plaque on it.

"Looks like it's here," he said and knocked.

"Let's hope we get some vital info then, eh?"

CHAPTER FIVE

Den filled some shelves out of boredom. He may as well shut up shop in a bit. The cold weather kept tourists away and the town's kids from venturing out for rock or toffees after school. With the predicted hurricane on the way, he reckoned people were staying indoors. Best thing to do, that. Saved you getting swept off your feet, didn't it.

While he stacked chocolate, he thought about the man who'd come in and bought that Mars and a magazine. Den had known him right from the lad being a kid, and he'd always put the shits up Den. He had weird eyes that seemed to see right into Den's soul and seek out his secrets. All right, Den had a few, but they weren't for the lad to know. Saying that, he wasn't exactly a lad now, was he. Blimey, he must be in his thirties by now. Had time really flown by so fast? Of course it had.

His son, Mark, was the same age. They'd gone to school together, had been best friends once upon a time. Not now, though. Not since the lad had shown signs of wanting to take a dark path, and nowadays he was always drinking in The Villager's Inn and going to the nightclub, rat-arsed even during the day sometimes.

People liked to come in and gossip.

Den's mind wandered, as it was prone to do lately, a downside of getting on in years. He recalled taking over this shop from his old man, and the pride he'd felt in continuing the family business had been like nothing he'd ever felt since. Sadly, his son didn't want it after Den popped his clogs, and the idea of it going to someone else, being sold off or even closed down, had Den's heart aching. Still, he'd rather that than force his boy to do something he didn't want to do.

Den had been so intent on running the shop, Mark hadn't arrived until Den was considered an 'old parent'. Despite that, Mark had done all right for himself, what with being a manager in the Nationwide just down the road. Den was made up for him and no mistake. No, Den wouldn't want him giving up his career to man a shop that was, if he were honest, on the verge of giving up the ghost. Summertime was all right, but in winter it became an abandoned relic, washed up and a far cry from its heyday where the paint had been fresher, the sign out the front brighter. The weather had got to it, as had all that salt in the air, and Den didn't have the energy or the money to get it sorted.

Someone appeared at the window, and Den glanced across. The lad stared inside, those fucking strange eyes of his boring into Den. The wind had really picked up, and it sifted through the kid's hair, pushing it to one side. Shuffling over to the door in his slippers, Den clicked the lock down and pulled at the blind so it hid the glass. Then he did the same with the window, shutting the creep out there, leaving the wind to buffet him every which way and hopefully send him home. Den shivered and, leaving the job of chocolate stacking for tomorrow, he put the float from the till in the safe then closed everything down.

With a Heineken can in hand, cold from the fridge, he went upstairs to put some dinner on. A bit of fish and chips wouldn't go amiss, and he popped them in the oven. There was no harm in having an early tea, was there. No, sometimes it was just the thing on a cold day like this. Shame his wife was no longer there to share it with him.

In the living room, he sat in his favourite chair and cracked open the beer, the job of lifting the tab more difficult now with his fingers being arthritic. Pain shot into his knuckles, and he closed his eyes until it passed, then had a good sip or two, contemplating whether he'd read tonight or watch a bit of telly instead.

Can clutched in both hands, he tipped his head back and dozed.

The lad was coming round for tea. Mark was excited, jumping here, there, and every-bloody-where, making a nuisance of himself on the shop floor. If Den didn't know any better, he'd say his boy had been scoffing some rock on the sly, had maybe sneaked a can of Coke while he was at it, too.

"Calm down," Den said. "You've not long seen him at school."

Mark zoomed between the racks in the shop, knocking off a bag of Golden Wonder.

"Pack it in now." Den walked over and picked the crisps up, putting them back in place. "Look, here he is."

Mark ran to the door and swung it open, and the lad stood there, no mum, no dad with him, and Den wondered what sort of parent would let a five-year-old kid go to someone's house by himself. Didn't everyone drop their children off? Mind you, everyone knew Den, so he supposed it wasn't so bad. The lad's mum, Regina, was a nice enough woman, if a bit harried since her husband had walked out. Maybe her new fella had put his foot down and said her son could walk there by himself.

"Come on in," Den said, holding the door open, seeing as Mark was struggling with the weight of it. "Upstairs with you. Mrs Simons has the food almost ready, so best you go now. You don't want it to go cold, do you?"

The lad came in and stared at the sweets, his eyes wide. "Can I have one of them?" He pointed a skinny finger at the pink sticks of rock.

"No," Den said. "Mrs Simons will have a treat for after tea. Ice cream or some such. She went next door to the parlour earlier, so I'm guessing I'm right. That'll be nice, won't it?"

The lad glared at him, his eyes going black, and a shiver spread from Den's spine to all over his skin, goosebumps sprouting. He rubbed his arms and shut the door, turning his back on him. Mark looked up, and Den smiled, hoping his face didn't betray how a young boy could unsettle him so much.

Something smashed behind him, and Den whipped round. A snow globe had fallen off the shelf. Water had splashed on the grey tiles, and the white spots of fake snow were scattered.

Den moved his attention to the lad, who smiled a creepy little smile.

"What happened there then?" Den asked, keeping his distance, unable to move forward to clear up the mess. It was stupid that the kid had him on edge like that, but there it was. He couldn't help how he felt.

"Dunno." The boy shrugged and grinned wider. "Why did you say no?"

Den blinked at the child's boldness. "Because I did."

"You shouldn't say no. Bad things happen when you do that."

Fucking hell. Den wasn't sure what to do. "Just go upstairs," he said, voice gruff. "The pair of you." He waved a hand for emphasis, wanting the lad gone and out of his sight.

Mark scooted from behind Den and legged it. The lad stayed where he was for a speck of time, still grinning, his eyes still black and weird. Then he ran to the back of the shop, to the door marked PRIVATE, and disappeared along with Mark.

Den had a feeling he'd regret having the lad here, but he brushed that idea away. It was daft to be afraid of a small boy.

Wasn't it?

CHAPTER SIX

Helena and Andy waited at the Talk Today door, and a woman opened up, smiling, her hair an outrageous red mop, her tortoiseshell-framed glasses round and taking up half of her elfin face. Blue eyes shone from behind them, and freckles stippled her nose, those on one cheek spotted like the Big Dipper constellation.

"Can I help you?" she asked, tilting her head. Her voice was the type to stop anyone stepping off the ledge — soft, kind, soothing.

Helena showed her ID. "I'm Helena Stratton, and this is my partner, Andy Mald. We're here to talk about Miss Greaves. I believe she works here."

"Oh. Okay." She appeared perplexed, a frown lasting only a few seconds, then she smiled. "Come away in then." She stepped back to allow them entry. "Just go up the stairs there, then turn left at the top. My office is right in front of you."

Helena climbed the steps, creeped out by the gloom and the smell of old furniture, kind of like the scent of a church. The walls were a grubby magnolia, a line of dirt from years of filthy hands touching them going up the middle where a handrail should be. She turned and entered the office, a cubbyhole really, one that wasn't big enough for all three of them without claustrophobia coming for an unwelcome visit.

Andy remained on the landing, then the woman joined him.

"Ah, it'll be cramped," she said, glancing at Andy as though it was his size that would create the problem. "Let's go into the other room. That's where the girls sit to answer the phones. There's only Val in there at the moment. Is that all right?"

"We'd rather speak to you alone," Helena said. "Then we can speak to Val."

"I wouldn't bother. She doesn't know Felicity."

"Sorry," Helena said. "I didn't ask what your name was."

"Janice. I'll just check whether Val is on a call." She popped her head into the next room and whispered, then opened the door wide. "Val will go into my office. It's been a quiet day."

I wish we'd had one of those.

Val, a timid-looking woman of about forty, brushed past with her head down, blonde hair fanning over her shoulders. She disappeared into Janice's office and shut the door. Janice held her arm out for Helena and Andy to go into the other, and they sat on black plastic chairs around a table with a computer and a phone on it. Another one the same was pushed against the far window.

"Now then, what do you need to know?" Janice asked, draping one leg over the other.

Keeping things in the present for now so she didn't tip Janice off, Helena asked, "When does Felicity work here?"

"Just Monday nights, six until midnight." Janice smiled. "She's a good sort, has a gentle manner about her, and that's what people need in times of distress, someone to keep them calm and help them through."

"How long has she worked here?"

"Oh, about two years. She had a traumatic experience herself, although she never has said what it was, so she wanted to give back, to help others. That's the sort of people we need here. Folks with empathy."

"What types of calls do you get?" Helena held a hand up to stop Janice answering. "Let me ask that again. Do you get any calls where the people ringing in would want to speak to the same person, and if they got someone else, they might get annoyed?"

"I wouldn't say annoyed." Janice twirled some of her mad hair around a finger. "More like panicked or upset, but we get them through that. Once they realise we're all nice and just want the best for them, they tend to calm down."

"So no one would have a grudge, say, if they couldn't speak to Felicity every time?"

"Has something happened? We're very careful not to let anyone know who we really are. We're just a voice at the end of the line. We actually use false names. This is a relatively small town, and anyone we know could be ringing. They could be embarrassed if they knew one of us recognised their voices."

"The same goes for the other way round, surely."

"Well, I suppose so…"

"Do you know of anyone who would have a grudge against Felicity?"

Janice laughed. "Good grief! No. She's a lovely person. Why?"

Helena was on the verge of telling her, what with her hypnotic, calming voice urging her to confess. Janice should have been a priest. Helena reckoned she could wheedle sins out of you in no time. "So you wouldn't say she had any enemies then."

"Not that I'm aware of. Again, why?"

Fuck it. "I'm afraid Felicity was murdered last night."

The words hung in the air, stark and blunt and shocking, and Janice's mouth flapped.

"P-pardon?"

"She was murdered." Helena hadn't liked saying it the first time, let alone having to repeat it. "A female was seen at her address. So, do you know of a woman who might be upset with her enough to do that?"

Janice wiped the tears that flowed down her cheeks, her hand shaking. "Absolutely not. She's a mouse, wouldn't hurt anyone. I don't quite understand this."

"Did she ever confide in you about anything?"

"No. Like I said, she had a bit of a traumatic time, but that was all she told me. I don't know any details."

"Okay, who else works here apart from Val?"

"A lady called Zoe Jacks. She does the night shift."

"I'll need her address."

"Of course. Shall I call Val in here? Then I can get Zoe's address for you from my office."

"That would be great, thanks."

While Janice left the room, Andy leant across and tapped Helena's arm.

"Doesn't seem like she's lying," he said.

"No, but then people are clever at hiding things when they want to." She ran her fingers through her hair. Having another murder case on their hands within days of the last one was likely to suck the strength out of her. They'd had no time to recover. She stifled a yawn.

Val scuttled in, all willowy limbs and flowing skirt, a hippie deep down if Helena was any judge. She floated to the chair Janice had occupied and gave a twitch of a smile.

"Hi, Val," Helena said. "Janice said you don't know Felicity, but we have to check these things."

"No," Val said, her voice so soft it drifted away immediately. "I've only lived here for a month. I moved from Liverpool."

"Oh, no accent?"

Val shook her head. "I'm an army brat. We didn't stay anywhere long enough for me to pick up any dialects."

"I see. So have you ever spoken to Felicity, or do you literally not know her at all?"

"I work days, and she works Monday nights."

"Have you ever had a call from anyone wanting to specifically speak to her?"

"No."

66

They weren't getting anywhere, and it was pointless continuing to ask questions.

"Right, thanks for your time."

Helena and Andy walked out, and Janice was waiting on the landing.

She handed over a slip of paper. "Here you go. Zoe knows Felicity. They were in the same class at school, so Zoe told me once."

"Great. Thanks for your time, and I'm sorry to have brought such bad news."

Janice nodded and led the way downstairs. She unlocked the door, and Helena slipped past her, Andy right behind. The whiff of kebabs wandered out of Chargrill as though wanting to entice them inside. Andy smiled and winked.

"We'd better not," she said. "One, they're bad for you, and two, we'll stink when we go to see Zoe." She pointed down the street. "Sandwiches. They're better, although that's debateable these days, given how long a loaf of bread lasts before it goes mouldy. You ever noticed that? Bloody preservatives."

"Can't say I have," Andy said. "The bread in my house isn't sitting there long enough to get mouldy. It's more at home in my belly."

She laughed and led him to the sandwich shop. Once she'd bought them ham salad baps and a carton of orange juice each, they returned to the car. Helena ate while staring at the back of a white Transit that was more beige than anything, given the amount of mud dust all over it. Someone had written in it: CLEAN ME, YOU LAZY BASTARD!

A fist had been drawn with the middle finger sticking up.

Charming.

The late lunch over with, she headed to the address. Like so many in Smaltern, Zoe lived on one of the estates where the sea was a backdrop. The climb up the cliff road tested the engine, and Helena shifted into a higher gear to help it to the top. Rain pelted it down then, splashing on the windscreen. She clicked the wipers on and leant forward a bit so she could concentrate better. Visibility was quickly poor, and she drove past the recreation ground slowly. The wind picked up, jostling the car, and it seemed the remnants of the hurricane from another country was upon them at last.

"Fuck it," she said, turning into the estate.

"Nasty gale," Andy said, rooting out a Werther's.

"Hmm. We're going to get soaked."

She parked at the kerb outside Zoe Jacks' and waited it out for a minute or so. With no sign of the rain letting up, she muttered an obscenity, then got out with her jacket over her head and dashed to the blue front door. Andy appeared beside her, and Helena knocked, thinking it would need a fair few taps before Zoe Jacks heard them. She'd probably be out for the count, what with working nights.

The woman must be a light sleeper, though. The door opened, and a thirtysomething stood staring at them, lilac fleece pyjamas on and black fluffy slippers. Then she glanced to one side at the weather.

"Fucking hell," she said, folding her hands over her stomach. "Look at that rain!"

Try being outside in it…

Helena smiled, feeling a right prat standing there beneath her jacket. She lowered it onto her body, shivering at the cold, wet dribble that sauntered down her back from the collar. ID out, she announced who they were and that they needed information on Felicity.

"Come in," Zoe said. "The bloody water's getting on my mat."

Inside, the door closing out the horrendous downpour, Zoe walked into a room on the left. A kitchen, with modern, high-gloss units in white and a matching dining table and chairs. The light-blue worktop appliances broke up the blank canvas, as did a parrot, its colours vibrant.

"Fack orf!" it said.

Vibrant vocabulary, too.

"Um, pardon the bird," Zoe said. "My friend thought it would be funny to teach it to speak."

Andy guffawed, and Helena smiled. A bit of levity in this otherwise upsetting and frustrating day might be just what they needed.

"Would you like a drink?" Zoe asked. "The coffee's not long percolated."

Helena spied a full carafe and nodded. "That would be lovely, thanks."

"Sit down then," Zoe said, sorting out the cups.

Helena and Andy sat closest to the far wall, a Monet print hanging there proudly as though it wanted them to believe it was the real thing. Helena watched Zoe for signs of unease. There were none whatsoever, unless she was good at hiding things. Her fluid movements gave the idea she had no secrets—none the police needed to know about anyway. Her blonde hair was shoulder-length and a little tousled, as if she'd recently got out of bed, although she seemed too alert for Helena's knock to have woken her, plus she'd been up long enough to brew coffee.

"So what can I help you with about Felicity then?" she asked, bringing all three cups over then going back to get the Sweetex and little individual cream pots, the sort supplied in travel lodges and the like.

Helena had seen them in B&M Bargains the week before last. Thirty-five pence a packet or something mad like that.

Concentrate.

Helena sorted her coffee out while Zoe sat, then stirred it and asked, "How well do you know her?"

Zoe looked at the ceiling. "Christ, now there's a question." She lowered her gaze and stared directly at Helena, green eyes glinting with trustworthiness. "I know her well from school, but not really since leaving. We didn't hang around with each other back then, and I didn't want to start once school ended. And I say I knew her well, but what I meant was I know *of* her. Sorry, but she's a bullshitter, and who wants to be mates with one of those?"

Helena loved Zoe's refreshing honesty, so she aimed to get more out of her. "What do you mean by bullshitter?"

Zoe sipped then put her cup back down. "She lied a lot. To the point where we wondered what the next cock-and-bull story was going to be. Stupid things, as well, like saying she'd had a scrap with someone, but when we asked that someone about it, there hadn't even been a scrap. It was like she said things to make herself look important or someone we ought to hang around with. It didn't. She just looked a dick."

Andy choked on his coffee.

"All right there?" Helena asked, holding back a smile.

He nodded, so Helena resumed her questioning.

"Do you remember if anyone got upset with her, either over the lies or anything else?" Helena drank a mouthful of coffee and almost said, "Mmm."

"Loads of people were pissed off at her. She did my head in. I swear, there was some form of crap coming out of her mouth every day. My old dear reckoned it was to make up for what had happened to her. She lost her mum and dad quite young, so maybe she was trying to get people to like her, so she had a family of sorts? I don't know. But she had her gran, so she wasn't totally alone."

Helena drank some more, hoping Zoe would babble into the silence.

She didn't.

Bugger.

"So if something terrible happened to Felicity, would you be surprised?" Helena asked.

Zoe blinked and frowned. "What, like someone punched her, stuff like that? No, it wouldn't surprise me. Unless she's stopped the fibs, I can well imagine someone clocking her one. I remember when she used to walk towards us, we'd say, 'Fucking Felicity'."

The parrot repeated it.

Zoe got up and covered its cage with a tartan blanket. "Sorry." She sat again and blew out a long breath. "*Has* something happened to her then? What, did she piss a bloke off?"

"A woman," Helena said.

"Doesn't shock me in the slightest." Zoe shrugged.

"Felicity was murdered last night." Helena waited for that to sink in.

Zoe's mouth dropped open, and her cheeks flushed, as red as a baboon's arse. "What?" Her eyelids fluttered as though she held back tears, but her eyes weren't wet. "Who would go *that* far?" All the negativity shown towards Felicity seemed to dribble out of her, and she rubbed her temples, eyebrows scrunching. "I don't get it." She stared at the table for a while, then looked up. "I mean, I know I said what I said, but *killing* her?" She shook her head. "No, I can't imagine anyone doing that. All right, Felicity is a bit of a silly cow, but... Why would anyone bump her off?"

"That's what we aim to find out," Helena said. "Do you know of any women who would want to do this to her?"

"No. Give her a mouthful, yes, but not that." She picked her cup up, hand shaking. "I can't get my head around this. I feel bad for talking that way about her now."

"Why? Just because someone's dead, doesn't mean your opinion should change." Helena smiled to take the harshness out of her words. "Death doesn't turn everyone into angels, you know, and you telling us what you did and how

73

you feel helps us a lot. We've heard she wouldn't hurt a fly, that she's nice, but your take is different."

Zoe held up a hand. "Now hang on, I never said she'd hurt anyone or she wasn't nice. She was just annoying as fuck, the silly bitch. Okay, she could have changed as she grew up, but I don't think a constant liar can stop doing it without help, do you?"

"Or at least being extremely strong in wanting to change their behaviour," Helena said. "When was the last time you saw her?"

"I have no idea, but it was in the nightclub. I remember wondering why Becky still put up with her. Must have been about a couple of months ago maybe? I don't see her at Talk Today if I can help it. She tends to use Janice's office on a Monday evening, so I go straight into the main room for my overnight shift and rarely see her. Crap, does Janice know? She thinks the sun shines out of her arse."

"Yes, we've just been there. That's where we got your address." Helena took another sip of coffee, glanced at Andy's cup to see how much he had left, then stood. "Thank you for your time." She held out a hand.

Zoe shook it somewhat awkwardly and rose. "I'll ask around a few of my mates, see if they've heard anything about Felicity and who she might have naffed off, if you like."

"Actually, if you could give me their names and numbers, one of my team can ring them."

Zoe walked out of the room, then entered with her phone in hand. She wrote down numbers and names on a pad from a drawer then handed the sheet of paper over.

"Thanks," Helena said.

As they made their way down the hall, the parrot shrieked, "Kill the bitch!"

A shiver whispered up Helena's spine. That damn bird had cobbled parts of their chat together and formed a sentence, that was all. Nothing to be creeped out about.

Back at the station, damp from her dart to and from the car in the rain, she handed the note to Ol and asked her and Phil to split the names between them and call all of Zoe's friends. She left them to it and, on the way to her office, was stopped short by Chief Yarworth calling her name.

What did *he* want?

She spun round, and he walked through the incident room towards her, chivvying her along until they reached her office. She went inside, and he followed, closing the door behind him. Helena strode to her desk then sat, wondering why he suddenly wanted to speak to her when he usually stayed holed up in his office and away from any 'drama' as he called cases.

He settled on the chair opposite, crossed his legs, and leant an elbow on the armrest.

"What can I do for you, sir?" she said.

"Go out on a date with me."

CHAPTER SEVEN

*M*um *was drunk again, and he was just about sick of it. No one else's mother seemed to need a bottle of Bacardi as a constant companion, but these days, she did. She weaved around the living room, the neck of the bottle held tightly, raising it to her mouth every so often then wincing while swallowing.*

Dad had left her a long time ago, and she had a boyfriend, one who expected him to do 'little jobs' he knew he shouldn't do. Like stealing money from Mum's purse or swiping the milk off the neighbour's doorstep. Only old Mrs Ritterwald had a milk delivery now, everyone else getting four-pint flagons from Waitrose instead. Sometimes Ritterwald even had orange juice outside her door, and he nicked that and all but kept it for himself. A treat.

"Eddie's going to leave me," Mum said. "Says I love the bottle more than him."

She loved the bottle more than anyone, even herself, but he didn't say anything. He was fifteen now, going on fifty, or so it seemed. She was wearing thin.

While she wittered on, he thought about the next job he had to do. It was bigger than usual, and scarier, but if he didn't do it…

Bad things always happened if you said no, that was what Eddie reckoned.

Going to tea at Mark's again would be great if he didn't have to nick stuff. He'd been going once a month for years, and apart from Den being there, he enjoyed it. He could pretend he was part of their family, although he didn't like Den.

The old sod had said no to him, and the time would come when he'd pay for that.

He wasn't sure how he'd steal what Eddie had asked for, seeing as Den was always behind the counter. Eddie wanted fags, and lots of them, and the job was to grab as many packs of two hundred as he could and throw them out into the back area, where Eddie would be waiting behind the brick wall at the end of the yard to collect them.

"I'm going to Mark's now," he said.

Mum ignored him, staggering about and crying, her wails getting on his wick. Tears streaked her gaunt face, the once rounded, rosy cheeks a thing of the past. He sighed and left her to it. After all, she wouldn't even notice he'd gone, nor would she care.

78

Why couldn't he have a mum who was interested in him? Why was he allowed to roam the streets alone, and when he came back in, he didn't get an ear-bashing?

He walked along, his mind a whirl of how things used to be and what they were like now. Once Dad had left and Mum relied on the drink to get her through, and Eddie had appeared to corrupt everything, life hadn't been the same. He didn't feel right inside himself most days, his happiness soured to spite, and Eddie's threats scared him into behaving the way he did. People said he was weird, a nasty little shit, but Eddie said you needed to be a little shit in order to get things done in this world.

Although Eddie was a bit of a mean git, he wanted to be like him.

So he'd do whatever Eddie told him and learn the ropes.

He trudged down the street where Den's shop was, the path streaming with tourists, the air filled with the scent of sunscreen. Old sol beat down on his head, and it itched. He gave it a good scratch and squinted at all the happy families, everyone laughing or smiling, some of the kids scoffing ice creams, giving themselves white, pink, or chocolate moustaches, beards even. Would Mrs Simons have something nice for afters again like they had last time? Sticky toffee pudding and custard? Jam roly poly?

His mouth watered, stomach griping – he hadn't eaten a thing since a slice of toast this morning, and he'd had to pick the mould off the crust. He turned into Den's, the shop packed with people grabbing sticks of rock, jars of brown-and-cream-striped humbugs, boxes of toffee, or browsing all the knickknacks they could take home to prove they'd had a family holiday. Something to brag about, wasn't it? How they'd want to brag about Smaltern was anyone's guess. He thought it was a shithole.

This was the chance he needed to get the fags, while Den was busy watching everyone with his eagle eyes to see if people stole anything.

A laugh burbled up at that, considering what he was about to do, and he scooted forward into the crowd, ducking to conceal his height, coming out the other side and dashing through the door marked PRIVATE. There were two more in the corridor that said the same, so he pushed one open and scanned all the storage boxes. Maltesers, Walkers, you name it, it was there. Farther along were the cigarettes, but before he grabbed any, he checked whether a key was in the back door.

It was.

He twisted it, shoved at the door, and propped it open with a small step ladder.

Eddie was out there, peering over the high wall.

Picking up a brown cardboard box labelled Superkings, he tossed it outside and kept going until the stack was gone. A noise in the corridor startled him, so he moved the ladder back, shut the door, and hid in the slot he'd created with the box removals.

"What the bloody hell did I do with that?" Den said, the sound of his scuffing footsteps loud as he came in. "Ah, there it is."

Waiting to make sure Den had gone, he peered around the box tower to his right. With the coast clear, he left the storage room and went through the second doorway, knocking to be let into the flat above. Mrs Simons answered, beamed a great big smile, and ushered him in.

"Can I have a drink?" he asked.

"Of course you can. I've got some Coke as a treat. How's that?"

He smiled.

Bad things wouldn't happen to Mrs Simons.

She hadn't said no.

CHAPTER EIGHT

Helena just about held in her laughter and kept the incredulous expression off her face as she stared across the desk at Yarworth. "A date?"

Rain smacked on the window, providing a dramatic form of music for this shitshow.

"Well, not exactly a date, more like as a companion," Yarworth said.

This was all a bit vague—and totally unexpected. And why use the word 'date'? Had he done it to see what her reaction would be?

"Um, Damien… Sir, this isn't something I'm comfortable with. I'm seeing someone, and going out with you wouldn't feel right. Unless it's for work, the answer is a definite no."

"It is for work," he said, giving her a smug smile.

Fuck.

"Sorry, but why would you call it a date then?" Was he intent on messing with her head or what? She'd had enough of men doing that to last a lifetime, thanks.

He shifted his foot. "Figure of speech."

"What's this all about?" She didn't have time for him piss-arsing around. Why didn't he just stay in his office and keep out of her face like he usually did?

"We have a few people visiting from the Met, potentials who applied to work here, and I wanted you to meet them, give me a nudge if you think they'll be any good." He stared at her with hope in his eyes. "We have two places available, and seven have been interviewed today. I can't seem to make up my mind, so I asked them out for a meal this evening to see how they fare in a more relaxed setting. What better way to get to know them than that?"

Helena couldn't think of anything dourer. Plus, she'd be letting Zach down, and they'd not long been a couple. She didn't fancy messing it up before it had really begun. What was more important? Work or life? Because of Uthway, she knew the answer to that. "I'd rather not, sir. If it isn't part of my job, then I don't need to do it."

He raised his eyebrows, wedged his elbows on the armrests, and steepled his fingers. He tapped the tips against each other, a tactic he always employed when he wanted to get his own way.

She wasn't going to back down. "Look, I'm not being funny, but I have a murder on my hands, all right? I need a break — today has been nonstop — and going out on a work-based evening isn't a break, is it," she went on.

"A murder? You've only just dealt with three others a few days ago."

If you were more on the bloody ball, you'd know about it already, but seeing as you tell me to just get on with it, why are you so shocked?

She shrugged. "I can't help the fact that some woman has decided to kill another. It's not like they ask for permission first. You know, 'Sorry if you're busy, but I really need to do this lady in.'" She sighed. "I might even have to work late, who knows. We have nothing to lead us to anyone yet, and there's so much sifting to do it isn't funny."

"In that case, I'll let you off," he said, standing.

That's good of you...

He smiled tightly, spots of colour deepening on the rounded balls of his cheeks. "I just thought it might be nice, that's all."

Nice?

"And we rarely communicate."

And who's idea was that?

"I'll see myself out." He left, closing the door quietly.

She blew out a long breath and stared at the ceiling. Why the hell he expected her to go with him on a casual interview was beyond her. He'd never asked her to get involved with that side of things before, so why start now? Did he think since she wasn't with Marshall anymore, he had an in?

I mean, a date…?

She shuddered at that thought and the memory of Marshall duping her the way he had. For the first couple of days after he'd been arrested, she'd asked herself whether she ought to do this job anymore. Her instincts had been way off with him, what with her not picking up on the fact he had a mental illness. All right, she'd gathered he was weird when he'd followed her places after they'd split, but the depths of his depravity hadn't been apparent at all until the bodies and the gifts he'd left behind had shown him for what he was. A monster.

She hadn't slept well, either, and after the days she'd had recently, a bit of relaxation in The Blue Pigeon with Zach was just what she needed. A nice meal, a couple of vodkas, and good company.

To get her mind off Yarworth's weird-arsed invitation, she went out into the incident room to find him talking to Ol. What the hell? Was he asking her to go with him now? Ol glanced around him at Helena, and Helena held her hands up in a gesture that said: *Don't do it if you don't want to.*

Ol looked up at him towering over her while she sat, appearing interested, being polite.

Helena shook her head and walked over to the whiteboard, studying it, trying to drown out the mumble of Yarworth's voice. She read the information, still none the wiser as to how to find this bitch who'd killed Felicity. Until forensics came back with any fingerprints or whatever, they had little to work with.

Her mobile rang, and she answered it.

"It's about work, don't worry," Zach said.

She hustled into her office anyway, closing the door. "What have you got for me?"

"A few things from the PM. She was struck, as well as being stabbed. Bruising came out on her stomach—what I could see of the skin anyway—so she was either punched before being stabbed, or in between each blade puncture. I've made out twenty-three individual slices, which, as you know, indicates anger for someone to keep stabbing that many times."

"Seems she knew her attacker. That's usually the case in situations like this." She sighed. "The problem is, she apparently kept herself to herself. She told her friend she'd been abducted by Uthway, can you believe, and after she escaped, she didn't mingle. So it'd have to be someone she worked with or from her past. I'm just about to go and speak to any colleagues at Smaltern Amusements before heading home. I can't believe how quickly the day has gone."

"Some of the stabs went through her back and into the bed," he said.

She swallowed and closed her eyes, imagining the blood-soaked mattress, the slits in it from where the knife had pierced. She cracked her eyes open and stared at the rain dribbling down the windowpane. *They're like tears.* A visual of Emma Walker in the bath assaulted her, the tulip Marshall had planted there sticking out of it. She blinked to get rid of it. "Blimey, that's someone with a serious rage problem. Anything else?"

"No sign of sexual interference, so that's something."

"Good. At least she didn't suffer that horror before he killed her. What about the strength needed to do this? Could it be a woman?"

"Of course. If someone's riled up enough, the strength comes. Other than what I've told you, there'll be nothing else until tomorrow. I'll carry on in the morning. It's been a bit of a difficult one, seeing as there's so much mess."

"Okay, still on for eight o'clock?"

"Yep, see you there."

"Hopefully — unless something else happens."

"Let's pray it doesn't then."

She ended the call, shoved her phone in her pocket, and returned to the incident room. Yarworth had gone, thank God, and Ol waved her over.

"All right?" Helena asked, searching Ol's face for any sign she was uncomfortable with having to speak to Yarworth about the 'date'.

"He tried getting me to go out with him tonight to some work thing, but I told him I was busy. Phil said he'd go, though, so that's sorted."

"How did Yarworth take that?"

"He looked a bit put out, to be honest." Ol lifted her shoulders.

"Bloody weirdo. If all he wanted was a 'companion', as he put it to me, what does it matter whether it's a woman or a man? It's a work thing. He doesn't need anyone dangling off his arm."

"I don't know, but I find him creepy, so no thanks." Ol gave an exaggerated shudder and hugged herself.

Best the subject was changed. "Have you found anything on social media at all?"

"No. Felicity's not even on it."

"Makes sense if she only had Becky and Jean. Has anything come back as to whether a phone was found at her place?"

"Yes, forensics are looking at it now."

"Good. What about Zoe Jacks' friends? Anything there?"

"I've only managed to get hold of two. Phil's spoken to one. None of them have heard anything about Felicity for years, so I'm assuming the rest will say the same. I'll keep trying them — they're probably at work and can't answer."

"Hmm. I need to nip to the amusement arcade with Andy to speak to the manager, so give it another hour here, then go home."

"Okay, guv." Ol twisted her seat round and picked up the phone.

Helena moved over to Phil. "Anything on CCTV or in the diary?"

"Nope," he said. "The nearest camera to Miss Greaves' home is at the local shops, and they're ten streets away. No one fitting the mystery woman's description was caught on camera, sorry, and all car number plates from shoppers have been verified as innocent people. The diary is a lot of the same thing, plus what she did that day, which is boring stuff. Nothing we can use."

"Thanks for trying." She walked to Andy's desk. "Come on, we need to be off."

They dashed across the car park, Helena dodging puddles and squinting to stop the rain getting in her eyes. In the car, Andy sighed and jabbed his seat belt on.

"What's up?" she asked, nosing the car onto the road.

"Yarworth."

"What about him?"

"He said someone new is joining our team."

"*What?*" Helena wanted to stop driving, but there were too many cars behind and nowhere to pull over. "He didn't fucking tell me that!"

"Yep, two new people. One will be coming our way."

"He implied they were coming here in general. I don't need another person on the sodding team. We do all right on our own, thank you." She was angry at not being told she'd be in charge of another person. Maybe he'd kept that info back because she'd refused to spy on the applicants over dinner. Shit, she wished she'd agreed to go now. At least she could have chosen the person herself. God knew who he'd pick. "Is Phil aware of that?"

"Yeah, I told him once Yarworth had buggered off, so he knows to opt for someone we'll all like. I made sure he got the gist of how important it is. Since I've stopped being a prat, we all get on well. It'd be a shame to mess that up."

"It would."

"I've got a confession." He fiddled with his fingers.

"What?" She parked outside the amusement arcade. With the windscreen wipers off, water floated down it in a complete sheet, rippling and opaque.

"I thought you were in on it," he said. "You know, sticking by what you said and asking for a new partner."

She faced him. "No. What I'm sticking to is us making a go of it, me and you as partners. I wouldn't go back on my word like that. I'm as pissed off as you, I can tell you that much."

"Sorry."

"Don't be. I'd have probably thought the same thing. Balls. All we can hope for is that we get a good worker. Besides, it isn't really going to affect me and you. We're out and about all the time. It's Ol and Phil who'll have to put up with them for the most part."

In a huff, she got out and waited for Andy under the black-and-red-striped awning so she wouldn't get any wetter. Together, they walked inside, the air musty and miraculously still holding the scent of the many cigarettes that had been smoked before the new law had come in years ago. The tangy smell of copper was prevalent. She headed towards the money exchange booth, which contained rows of coins in orange slots and an old gal who had worked there so long she might have grown roots in the chair.

Holding her ID up to the plastic shield, Helena waited for the woman to leave the booth.

"Glen!" she shouted, shoving little fists on her hips. "Come and watch the money for a minute or two."

Glen appeared, all six feet of him, his gait loping, his shaved head and features giving him the look of that weird bloke in *The Munsters*. He slid into the booth and locked himself in.

"How can I help you?" the woman asked, her voice high and screeching.

Helena stared down at her, trying not to wince. "What's your name, please?"

"Betty Crocker," she said and wheezed out laughter. It turned into a cough, and she thumped her chest, eyes watering. "Barbara Cooper really. I do like a bit of a joke."

"Is there somewhere private we can talk? We're here to discuss Miss Greaves." Helena lifted her eyebrows.

"I've got an office, but it looks like the arse end of that bloody hurricane ripped through it. If you don't mind a bit of mess, be my guest." She pointed at a black door beside the booth with NO ENTRY on a gold plaque, then toddled over there. Door open, she held it back, wrinkled hands splayed on it.

Helena and Andy went inside, and Barbara hadn't been wrong. The place was a shit tip. Bills and papers covered the desk, the keyboard buried beneath, only one corner of it visible. The computer monitor was one of those old ones with a sloping back, the white casing grimy with age and possibly cigarette smoke. Cardboard boxes were stacked along the left wall, multi-coloured fluffy toys for the grab machine peering out of the top one, an arm here, a leg there, and an assortment of heads, ears, black plastic noses, and googly eyes. On the floor beside the doorframe, various small trinkets filled a red-and-white checked washing bag, the sort you took to the laundrette.

All in all, it was chaos.

Barbara let the door go and flopped into the only chair, the black leather ripped, cracked, and worn. "Is she coming in any time soon? I mean, I have people lining up to work here, so she really ought to count herself lucky she has a job."

"Unfortunately not," Helena said. "Had Miss Greaves ever confided in you at all?"

Barbara barked out a laugh. "Not fucking likely. She does her job then goes home. Hardly speaks to me."

"And what exactly did she do here?"

"Mans the money, refills the grabby machine, puts coins in the slider games. You know the ones? You put your money in, and the slider pushes it forward? You might win a keyring if you're lucky."

"Yes, I know what you mean." Helena wasn't there to talk about how the pissing amusements operated, and she sensed she'd get ratty soon. "Do you know whether she had any trouble from customers — females in particular?"

"Nope. She's quiet as a bleeding mouse, that one. Not any trouble — until today, that is. Her not turning up means I have to sit in that booth, and it's claustrophobic. Glen's not much cop at counting, but I had to get him in there, otherwise I can't talk to you. And as for that Becky just swanning off the way she did once that copper had come to see her…"

"I'm afraid Felicity was murdered last night."

"Murdered? What the fucking hell?" Barbara grabbed the desk for support with one hand, and several papers sailed off and landed on the floor, one covering her shoes. "I thought that fella was caught!"

"It's a different killer, Barbara."

"Gawd blimey. Why would anyone want to kill her? All right, she's a bit of a wet blanket, but that's no reason, is it?"

"No. Wet blanket?"

"Oh, always off in her head, she is." Barbara pointed to her temple and tapped it. "Jumpy as well. Say boo, and she'd crap herself. Sorry, but the thought of her having enemies is laughable. Talking of boo, she wouldn't say it to a goose."

"It's really important for you to think now as to whether anyone would have been upset by her at work."

"There's no one."

After a few more questions and nothing of value surfacing, Helena had a quick word with Glen. It was obvious he didn't have a clue as to who would have killed Felicity, spluttering about how he'd barely spoken to her because she hadn't seemed to like him.

They left the arcade, and Helena dropped Andy home. Then she went to her house to have a nice vodka with ice while she had a bath.

She had a proper date to go on.

CHAPTER NINE

I am God; you will obey.

Helena shuddered. Emilija, the Lithuanian woman who'd escaped from Uthway's place in Lime Street, had told her that was what the symbols carved into the dead bodies meant. The women he'd discarded as not being good enough to sell on in the sex-slave trade had been murdered, their bodies left for Helena to find, the symbol a mystery, a warning to the other captives. That was all she'd had to go on in the beginning, but a tip-off had come in from a neighbour in Lime Street who'd got suspicious about the amount of activity in Uthway's den — men going in and out during the day, and dark figures doing much the same at night. A white van also appeared, always after midnight, and shadows in the shape of people were taken inside.

And the caller had also said a naked woman had run out of the house and disappeared into the trees during the day.

That had been what Helena had needed – a place to check out, somewhere to watch. After Emilija had been questioned, Helena went off on her own, leaving Andy behind in the incident room, telling him she needed to go and post a parcel and she wouldn't be long.

She threw protocol out of the window and headed for Lime Street. She positioned herself across the road, hiding in amongst the trees and bushes. It was daytime, so she'd be safe. Telling herself she'd just watch for an hour, she settled down on her knees, binoculars in front of her eyes.

Ah, there were the men – well, two at any rate – talking out on the path. She was too far away to hear what they were saying, but the gestures and head shaking told her something was bothering them. Probably Emilija's escape. If one person could get away, what was to stop someone else bolting? She imagined them saying that.

Had any others got away, too?

Then the men went inside for a moment and came out again with several others, closing the front door. All of them walked away from the house in different directions.

Were only the captives inside now?

She hadn't actioned a unit to come and storm the place yet. She'd told Andy she'd do it once she'd sent her parcel. She hadn't passed on the new information *about Emilija's escape to Yarworth because he never wanted to know about cases until they were over. No, she'd just come straight here, the late-afternoon sun still as hot as it has been that morning when Emilija had broken free.*

While she watched for signs of more activity, she thought about her interview with Emilija.

"Was it only you who got away?" Helena had asked.

"I don't know. I was busy thinking about myself. Cruel. I was cruel not to help the others."

Helena had reached out and taken Emilija's hand and squeezed it. "You were fighting to survive. Don't blame yourself." She'd paused, then, "Do you know any of the others' names?"

Emilija had shaken her head. "We were not allowed to say. If we did, they would kill us. There were men, too. Young men. Aged around eighteen, but just two of them. The rest were women."

"Okay." Helena had sighed. "What happened? How did you get away?"

"There were so many of us in that room. We were packed in. I wondered if they even knew how many. They could have forgotten to count, I do not know, but that was what went round in my head – they do not know the numbers. Somebody came in, one of the big men, the nasty one, then he was called away by a shout. He shut the door, but it did not lock."

"So you took the opportunity to leave?"

Emilija had nodded. "I did. I said to the others it was our chance, but they were too scared. Many said they would stay there. A couple said they might run, too. We had to whisper in case we were heard. But I could not stay. I did not want to be raped again." She'd lowered her head. *"I did not want to be sold to a rich man who would use me like that. So I got up and opened the door. It hurt — my body was so sore from not moving much."*

Helena had let go of her hand and pushed Emilija's cup of tea towards her.

Emilija had ignored it. "I walked out into a hallway, and the front door was right there. It was not locked either, and that was stupid of them to do that. I slipped into the front garden, and the light hurt my eyes. The sun was shining. I guessed it was morning. I made out some trees opposite. I ran there and kept running, through the woods to the other side, and then someone called out. I was afraid it was them, the men, but it was a lady, and she had a dog. She called the police." Emilija had shivered. "As you know, I had no clothes on. It was not even embarrassing. I had been seen and touched by so many that... It did not matter anymore." She'd picked up her tea and swallowed some.

From there it had been a case of Helena collecting Emilija, ensuring she was seen by a doctor, that she was examined using a rape kit, and that she'd had a shower and a clean change of clothes.

And then the interview had come.

Helena blinked away the memory and concentrated on the Lime Street house. The window beside the front door had been whited out with some kind of substance applied in circular swirls, the sort used when people were decorating and didn't want anyone nosing in. Emilija had said sheets of wood had been secured over the glass inside, creating a strange darkness, everyone held there transformed to nothing but deep shadow-shapes.

"Where did they take you when you had to leave the room?" Helena had asked.

"Upstairs. They 'tested' us to see if we could be sold."

"Tested?" Helena had had an idea of what she'd meant but had to be sure.

"Raped."

Helena had it in mind to watch for a short while now, then call in surveillance. Once everyone was in place, they'd gain entry, and the rest would be history. She wondered why she'd opted to watch alone first. Why hadn't she followed protocol?

Because she'd followed her instincts, her base need to rescue the people inside that room herself. And that was just stupid. One person couldn't do that. She needed her team, the other officers.

She was yanked from behind, a hand clamping over her mouth, and dragged backwards. With no time to cry out, she fought to break free, glancing over her shoulder to see who had grabbed her. A big man, someone too big to shake off, and the realisation that she'd fucked up big-time slammed into her.

Andy's repeated warning floated into her mind: *You can't be a lone vigilante; it doesn't work like that.*

No, it didn't, and there she was, being hauled through the trees then thrown into the back of a white van — the van that had undoubtedly been used to ferry the abducted men and women to a place where unimaginable things happened.

Helena shot up in the bath, her heart hammering, her vodka glass floating in the water down by her feet. She'd bloody well fallen asleep, and her mind had taken her back in time, tormenting her with everything she'd done wrong, when all she'd wanted was to do everything right.

She shoved the hideous memories away — she couldn't keep dwelling on how she'd fucked up. Instead, while she washed her hair, she reminded herself of what had transpired after she'd been taken. She'd later been told Andy had stepped up and actioned the arrests at Lime Street, but with Emilija breaking out, the men had left the house to look for her, one of them finding Helena instead.

How dumb had she been to think she could deal with it all by herself?

Arrogant, more like.

She finished her bath and got out, wandering into her bedroom to dry off then sling some clothes on — skinny jeans, a fluffy pink jumper — and dried her hair in seconds, which reminded her of how long it used to be, how she'd had it chopped off as soon as she could after she'd jumped off that cliff into the sea and found help.

Funny how a woman exercising her dog had helped Helena, the same as what had happened with Emilija. The similarity, the poignancy of it hadn't registered then, when Helena had walked out of the sea onto the shingle, waving the lady down.

She shivered and remembered Uthway curling her hair around his fist while he—

No.

She stared at herself in the mirror and willed a smile onto her face. It was over, all of it, and although guilt remained about her actions, how if Andy hadn't thought on his feet and had given the word to go to Lime Street and rescue those poor people, they could have been moved on, sold, and living lives with strangers who took whatever they wanted, when they wanted.

No men had been apprehended, only the captives had been found.

So had Felicity escaped at the same time as Emilija?

She sighed at it all.

Don't beat yourself up about it.

She tried. Every day she tried not to do that, but at some point in every twenty-four hours, that guilt prickled, usually in her sleep. Maybe it always would.

"Make it better by never doing anything like that again," she said to the reflection of a woman who no longer looked like her.

That's because she isn't me. The woman I know died in that storage container.

She brought herself fully into the present and made an effort with mascara and even created a style to her hair instead of just leaving the short strands to rest flat. It was time to start living in the now, not in the past.

And with that thought in mind, she left the house and walked to The Blue Pigeon.

CHAPTER TEN

Den woke to the sound of tapping downstairs. He got up as quickly as he could, his back giving him gyp, nerves biting at the base of his spine. Shuffling over to the window that faced the street, he found it was deserted, as it would be at this time, the wind gusting up the road, howling away and tossing a ball of paper around. He opened the window and peered down. No one stood at the door, and anyway, he'd shut up early, so when the blinds were drawn, that was tough tits. All the locals knew that.

He closed the window and ambled into the kitchen. His nap had been longer than he'd wanted, and a few of the chips were burnt on the edges, verging on black at the tips. The fish was all right, though, nice and crispy, so he took it out of the oven and dished it all up, sprinkling salt and vinegar.

Back in his chair, a tray on his lap, he tucked in, dipping a chip into the splodge of Daddies brown sauce he'd squirted on the side of his plate.

Halfway through his meal, he paused. What the bloody hell *was* that noise? He waited for it to come again and, yep, there it was, maybe the rattling of a door handle. It could be the wind doing it, but it was more likely to be children playing silly buggers.

"Bleeding kids," he muttered, dumping the tray on the coffee table then pushing to his feet. His knees cracked, and he winced.

I bet they're fucking about in the yard.

Downstairs, he walked to the back of the storage room. The rear door stood ajar, moving back and forth in quick, wide arcs, and he frowned, trying to think whether he'd locked it or not. Sure he had, he shrugged and moved to close it. The wind shoved it as far open as it would go, the handle smacking into a tower of boxes containing jars of old-fashioned sweets and leaving a dent. Annoyed in case one of the jars had cracked, Den stepped to the threshold and peered outside, his hair lifting at the front from a stout whoosh of breeze. The *shh* of a cardboard carton sliding had him turning to catch it before it fell, but instead of being met with that, a blonde woman stood there, all in black, glaring at him.

"What the hell are you doing in here?" Den asked, outraged at the intrusion, the hairs on the back of his neck rising.

The wind gave an ominous howl.

"You said no," she said in the same voice as that lad who had always given him the creeps.

Den blinked. "What?" The memory of the time the lad had asked for a stick of rock thundered through his mind. He shivered. Was that what this was all about? And if it was the same kid, why did he look like a woman now?

"You heard me," she said. "I doubt you're fucking deaf yet, old man."

She thumped Den in the stomach. He doubled over, letting out an *oof*, clutching his midriff, eyes watering from the pain, and he scrunched them shut, telling himself to stand upright, to run, but he didn't manage it. The slam of the door snapping against the frame had him wondering if it was the woman leaving or the wind tugging at it. Then the noise of the key scraping in the lock told him the truth.

Just about to lift his head, Den said, "What do you want?" If it was money, she was shit out of luck. He didn't make much out of season, and the safe only had the day's takings in it and the float, which was about sixty quid.

107

"Bad things happen when you say no," the woman said behind him.

It's not a woman, it's the lad.

Confusion crept into Den's mind, obliterating every coherent thought, and a buzzing set up in his ears from fear, a million bees. Something smacked him on the back of the head—Christ Almighty, that hurt—and he went down on his knees, the hard floor unforgiving on his old-as-dirt bones. He stopped himself from crying out, not wanting the woman-lad to know he'd hurt him, his pride still intact despite the circumstances. Pain lanced into his thighs, streaking up to flood into his hips, settling there as spearing jolts. His dentures came loose, and he clamped them together to stop them from shooting out.

"I'm Bête Noir, and you will understand what that stands for soon."

Bête Noir? What the hell is that?

"You're about to learn a thing or two," the woman-lad said and gripped the back of Den's jumper.

She pulled it so hard the neckline dug into his throat. He couldn't breathe.

Hauled to his feet, Den opened his eyes and blinked, a blinding headache blooming at the back of his skull, pulsing and jabbing pinprick sensations on his scalp. The neckline loosened, and he sucked in a huge breath, his lungs thanking him for it.

What was he going to learn? And what did it mean: *bad things happen*? What, was Den going to get beaten up now, all over a stick of ruddy rock? All because he'd said no to the lad having one? Hadn't he given him enough over the years? Food from his table, fizzy drinks from the shop fridge?

He opened his mouth to ask those questions, but the woman-lad shunted him forward, kneeing him in the arse, out of the room and up the stairs, Den tripping every few steps, his slippers gaining no purchase on the worn carpet. His chest hurt with a tightness he'd experienced before, when he'd had a mild heart attack after his wife had died, the shock of her death too much for him to handle.

What was going to happen to him now? Would he have a bigger attack and die?

And… Oh God. What about Mark? He was due round later for his weekly visit. Eight o'clock he always turned up, and never a moment sooner or later. What if Den snuffed it and Mark found him?

"My son…" he managed as he was dumped in his chair, which reared back on its hind legs from the force. It plopped down again, and Den was almost launched out of it.

"What about the prick?"

Den stared up at a kid he'd always known would turn into a wrong sort, except that female face was disconcerting, throwing Den off. He'd told Mark to keep away from him once they'd left school. He had no joy in being right, in predicting the future for this kid, now a man in what Den finally gathered was a mask and a wig, looming over him with an extra-long knife in a steady, black-gloved hand.

Christ...

"He'll be here soon," Den said, wishing his voice hadn't wobbled. Would the idea of Mark arriving put a stop to this? Scare him off?

"Best I work a bit quicker then, eh?"

It was so strange for a male voice to come through the slit between the female lips. He had no time to ponder on that anymore.

The blade seared a wicked, agonising path through Den's gut.

"One," Bête Noir said.

He stared at Den, who appeared shocked to see a knife handle sticking out of his belly. The old man's face turned white, and his eyes watered. His fingers fluttered on the armrests, as though he wasn't sure what to do with them—use them to take the knife out or leave them where they were, as ineffectual as butterfly's wings.

Decisions, decisions.

The stupid bastard's birds were coming home to roost, weren't they, squawking and flapping, ready to peck him with their vicious beaks.

Face sweating from the mask, he wanted to wipe the dampness away but didn't dare waste precious minutes. He reckoned that line about Mark coming by was a desperate attempt to stop him from doing what he wanted. Well, Den had found out it hadn't worked, but it was best to get a move on, just in case.

He punched Den in the stomach a few times, either side of the knife handle, just so the git knew what it felt like to always have a tummy that hurt from anxiety. Living a life with it constantly there since Eddie had moved in had been one of the worst aspects of his days, even more than doing the little jobs, more than Mum being a vibrant star in his life once upon a time then dissolving into a black hole when Eddie had got his feet firmly under the table.

Anger surged, and he socked Den in the face, knocking him out. Den's head drooped to the side, one cheek squished against his shoulder, mouth sagging. Blood trickled out of his nose, from his split lip, as well as from the knife wound. The old man was getting what he deserved, getting what Eddie had meted out a few years ago, except Eddie hadn't used the knife properly, the dumb fuck.

He'd side-stepped, anticipating the stab, then decked Eddie and warned him that if he ever tried to touch him again, he'd kill him.

Eddie had tried a couple of months later, of course he had.

And I kept my promise.

Eddie's bones were probably still at the bottom of the sea, his flesh gnawed away by greedy fish.

Snapping out of the memories, he walked into the kitchen and pulled out the clothes airer from beside the fridge. He'd seen Mrs Simons putting it away once. He took it into the living room, placing it to one side of the chair, then went into the yard to cut off some of the large roll of plastic sheeting. Upstairs, he draped some of it over the airer, creating a shield. With Felicity, he'd had more time and foresight, and he'd taped the sheeting up on the ceiling and the wall so the blood hadn't gone all over the place, but if Mark really was due, there were scant minutes in which to finish the job, so he couldn't risk attaching it to the ceiling here. He'd take it with him to burn in his back garden afterwards, like he'd done before.

Next, he dragged over a couple of dining chairs and positioned them on the other side of Den, their backs to his chair arm. He covered them in sheeting, memories sifting in from when he'd used it while killing Eddie in the garage. That instance he'd protected the walls and the floor with it, but that was a luxury he couldn't afford now. These shields would have to do, would serve the purpose of letting the police know it was the same killer. With minimal blood surrounding the chair, just like Felicity's bed, they'd know.

He wanted recognition for all the years he'd suffered. He needed to be important. To have people acknowledge that a bad upbringing resulted in this…this carnage.

Knife handle gripped in his fist, he pulled the blade out of Den. Blood gushed, and he stared at the river of it spreading, tainting the old duffer's cream shirt, its journey moving south to soak his light-brown trousers. Fascinated, he gazed at Den's face, at his eyes opening, his mouth gaping to allow a long, drawn-out wail to pass between his lips.

Noisy bastard.

Then he stabbed, twenty-two times, making the total twenty-three.

Twenty-three. One for every year he'd suffered having Eddie in his life.

Mark had left earlier than usual so he could get home to watch a programme that started at nine. He walked round to the shop's back yard, taking his keys out of his pocket. He tried inserting one into the lock, but it wouldn't go all the way in. Tutting, he peered into the hole. A key was already in there from the other side. Dad had obviously forgotten to take it out. He pulled his mobile from his pocket and dialled Dad's number, but there was no answer, only the trill of the rings sounding in his ear and also feebly from a distance, inside the building. Dad had probably fallen asleep in his chair, the daft sod.

With no key for the front of the shop—and it would have the chain and bolts across on the inside anyway—he looked around the yard for something to poke the key through with. A slim stick rested on the path beside a roll of plastic sheeting and a backpack. Had Dad forgotten those, too? And what the buggering hell would he need the plastic for?

Mark grabbed the stick and jabbed it into the lock. It took a minute or two, but the jangle of the key dropping on the floor inside proved it had been worth the effort.

He entered the storage room, stooping to pick up the key, then locked the door. In the hallway, he paused. Movement above creaked, as though someone prowled the flat, and he called out, "Dad? It's only me."

Footsteps. Hurried. Faster than Dad's. Scuttling.

Mark frowned. Was someone else up there? Maybe one of his bridge mates had popped round for a bevvy. Mark made his way to the foot of the stairs, and someone stood at the top, obscured by bundles of scrunched-up, red-smeared plastic. Paint? Was Dad finally tarting the flat up? It was about time. The shoes were visible, modern black trainers, not something Dad would wear, and the bottoms of the legs sported black jeans.

"All right, mate?" Mark asked, going upwards. "If you don't mind me asking, who are you?"

Whoever it was didn't reply, and as Mark reached the ninth step, he was shoved, the plastic crinkling against his belly. A split second was all it took to glance down at his white T-shirt stained with faint red smudges, then he was falling backwards, arms windmilling, his feet leaving the solidity of the steps. He crashed down, each riser smacking into his back—that'd leave a few bruises—and he landed on the floor below, stunned. He gazed up, staggered by the fact they'd bloody pushed him. The person, still hidden behind the plastic, descended, and Mark struggled to get up, disorientated, his whole body aching from his tumble.

"What the fuck did you do that for?" he asked.

The plastic drifted to settle at Mark's feet, and he stared at the woman who'd held it. What the hell was going on?

"Bête Noir. That's my name." She had a sodding strange voice, part gasp, part rasp.

"Bête Noir? I've not heard of you. What are you doing here?"

"Never you mind. Bit of bad luck for you turning up early, eh?"

Mark recognised the new voice, one he'd heard too many times to count, and his guts churned. "You!" he said on a ragged breath.

What was with the hair and the different face? And that stupid name?

"Yeah, it's me. I'm glad you're here. Saved me a bit of hassle, you have."

A knife appeared in his old friend's hand, bloodstained — what the fuck? Dad? — and Mark gawped in horror as it came towards him in slow motion, unable to process what was happening quickly enough.

It entered his stomach.

"One…"

It pulled out then sliced in again.

"Two…"

Mark wrenched himself out of his stupor at five stabs, concentrating on trying to get up to defend himself, managing to rise to his knees, his hands ineffectual in batting at the mad figure in front of him. A fist connected with his stomach, bringing on such horrendous pain and blood loss he flopped backwards, landing sprawled on his side. More stabs and punches came, into his belly, more blood spurting—it pumped out with the frantic beating of his heart, and Mark swore it stretched the stab wounds wider every time it exited.

"Six, seven, eight…"

His head swam. So many stabs now.

"Twenty-three."

Then his attacker stopped, scooped up the plastic bundle, and walked through the doorway that led to the corridor behind the shopfront. Mark watched him with blurred vision. His head lightened, his guts on fire, and his strength seeped out of him. He thought of his wife and their baby at home, and that gave him enough energy to get his phone out, fumbling to access the keypad, and call for an ambulance.

The dispatcher fired off questions, and he told her he'd been stabbed and where he was, then words failed him. His mind failed, too, and he couldn't compute what he was being asked. He dropped the phone and would have pressed his hands to his belly to stop the blood flow if he had enough strength, but it was ebbing away faster now, as were any comprehensible thoughts.

He closed his eyes, vaguely aware of the blood still pulsing from his wounds, and he knew, as sure as he knew his name, that he wasn't going to make it.

He was hacked off at Mark being early, at not being able use his plastic sheeting when he'd offed him. The police wouldn't know the same person had killed Mark and Den now, for fuck's sake.

Trust Mark to be the one to mess it all up.

He stormed out of the storeroom and into the yard, stuffing the soiled sheeting into a black bag he'd brought along just for that job. It had Mark's blood on the outside of the bundle, and that just plain pissed him off. Then he removed his gloves and shoved them and the knife in with the plastic. Taking off his wig and mask, he put them into the backpack, a few streaks of blood clinging to the blonde hair. He turned his hoodie inside out so the red side showed, put it back on, gathered his belongings, and exited the yard. He sauntered down the alley and into the maze of streets beyond the back of the shop, darkness cloaking him, giving him anonymity.

Once he got home, he'd soak the knife in bleach, shampoo the wig, and put his clothes in the machine on a hot wash. Christ, Mark wasn't supposed to have been killed until tomorrow. The turn of events bugged him.

He shrugged. Did it really matter? No. No, it didn't.

CHAPTER ELEVEN

Helena had decided not to have any alcohol, seeing as Zach had opted for a Diet Coke. She'd sipped hers over the course of an hour, and Zach stood at the bar now, getting another round in. Her dinner had settled heavy in her stomach—serves herself right for choosing a steak and ale pie with chips, peas, and thick gravy—and she leant back in her carver chair, tempted to unbutton her jeans and let her food baby flop out.

Her phone warbled in her jacket pocket, so she tugged it out, hoping it wasn't work. Unfortunately, it was. Clive's name showed on the screen, and she wondered why he'd be ringing her. He was a uniform and not someone she dealt with unless it was at a scene.

"Hello?" she said.

"Hi, guv. Sorry to ring you, but I'm at a murder location, and I think this is linked to the other one."

"What makes you say that?" she asked.

"They've been stabbed in the stomach. Father and son, and I'm gutted because I know them both. I went to school with the son, Mark Simons. The other victim is Den Simons."

"The owner of that little shop?" Helena felt a bit sick. Who the hell would want to kill Den? He was a lovely old fella, and everyone knew him.

"Yes. A call came in from Mark. He said he'd been stabbed, so I went out to have a look. The back door of the shop was unlocked, but the front was secure. I went in and found Mark at the bottom of the stairs that lead up to the flat. I checked him for a pulse, and he was deceased, so I went upstairs and stopped at the living room door. Den was dead in his chair. I left the premises and I'm outside in the back yard."

"Blimey, sorry you had to see that on top of finding Felicity. I'll be there in a few."

"All right, guv. I called it in, and SOCO are on the way."

"Okay. Zach's with me, so I'll let him know. Speak in a bit."

Zach walked over, minus drinks. "Just had a call from the front desk."

"I've had one from Clive. Good job we only had a Coke really, isn't it." She could ignore the vodka she'd poured earlier. It had all spilt in the bath anyway when she'd fallen asleep.

He nodded.

"Can you drop me home so I can get my car?"

"Of course."

In Zach's, she rang Andy and said she'd be with him inside ten minutes. Zach pulled up outside her house.

"Thanks for a lovely evening," she said. "Shame it was cut short."

"It is, but it's the nature of our jobs. At least in this relationship, we understand the downside of it and won't give each other any grief."

"There is that." She leant across and kissed his cheek, then got out, waving as he drove away. In her vehicle, she made the journey to Andy's with the victims on her mind. Were the murders related like Clive thought? Just because they'd been stabbed, didn't mean it had been the same killer.

She arrived at Andy's, and once he was in the car and had buckled up, she told him what had happened.

"Fucking hell," he said. "Another person killing straight after Marshall is a bit much to take in. I was just thinking that before you rang."

"Maybe the Walkers being murdered gave them the courage to do the same thing. It doesn't take much to set some people off. It's all everyone has been talking about, and with it being on the news…"

"Hmm." Andy got a Werther's out and popped it in his mouth. "Want one?"

"No, thanks. I've got a belly full of pie. Couldn't eat another thing."

She drove down the street where Den's was, and a lump in her throat had her swallowing to force it away. It reduced in size a bit but continued to make its presence known. This little shop had been here forever, the place to go and get your treats and whatnot. It was more than a newsagent's, with the holiday trinkets, rock, and jars of sweets. People flooded there in the summer, buying gifts to take home with them once their holiday had ended. There were other places that were similar, but none had the lovely Den behind the counter, giving you a smile and a bit of a chat.

No shop would ever have him serving people anymore.

Damn it.

She blinked the nostalgia and emotions away and parked behind Clive's police car, the SOCOs' van behind it, two officers in white garb walking from the rear of it and down the alley to get to the back of the shop, carrying their bags.

"Fucking hell," she said. "This is surreal. I mean, Den..."

"Isn't it just." Andy clicked the button to release his seat belt, the Werther's clacking against his teeth as he shoved it around in his mouth.

They got out, and Helena glanced about for Zach's car. It was a few vehicles up, and he wasn't inside it. She led the way to the yard, and Clive stood by the open back door, the spill of light from indoors coming out to bathe one side of him in a white-tinged radiance.

"Are you okay?" she asked, concerned he'd now been the one to find three bodies. That sort of thing could affect you badly.

"Bit shaky. I didn't expect them to be in such a state. I imagined just one stab." Clive rubbed his forehead then held out the scene log.

Helena signed it. "So it's more then." She handed the log to Andy.

"A fair few." Clive sighed.

"Might well be linked to Felicity Greaves' murder, like you thought. We'll soon know. Zach's in there, I take it?"

"Yes, guv." Clive took the log from Andy. "You'll need to steady your nerves. It isn't pretty." He jerked his head at the door.

"Will do."

She put booties and gloves on, and Andy did the same, Helena wondering why the back door was open and whether whoever it was had come in while the shop had still been trading, hiding out upstairs until Den had finished work.

She walked inside, Andy behind her, and had a nose about. The storeroom looked much like she imagined it should, boxes in stacks, a table and chair at the end with papers, a pen, and a small laptop on it. She shook her head and went out into a corridor, turning and entering the shop. Nothing had been disturbed as far as she could gather, so she asked one of the SOCOs working in there where the stairs were for the flat.

"The door beside the one for the storage room, guv."

"Thanks."

She went there and pushed it, momentarily shocked at the sight of a thirtysomething man at the bottom, even though she'd been told he was there. Yes, he'd been stabbed, multiple times, and blood was everywhere, totally different to Felicity's bedroom. The stairs, the walls, the banister rails, the carpet on the lowest three steps, although oddly, at his feet, there was a clean patch. A SOCO stood beside the body, taking pictures, and he glanced at her, his eyes kind over the top of his face mask.

"Two seconds," he said, "and I'll be out of your way. I've already done upstairs."

The stench of blood was horrific, and the pie in Helena's belly seemed to swirl. She swallowed and looked away from the body to Andy. "I think we need suits on, don't you?"

They'd get blood on their clothes if they weren't careful.

He nodded, and they went back to the storeroom, taking an outfit each from the box in the yard. Clive remained quiet while they dressed, staring at his feet, probably seeing the carnage in his mind all over again.

Back at the foot of the stairs, the photographer had gone, and Helena managed to skirt around the body without stepping in too much blood, missing the lowest stairs, and hefting herself up onto the fourth—a bit of a strain on the old thigh muscles. At the top, she took in the sight of SOCO in each room, then walked into the living room where Tom waved from doing a fingerprint sweep on the windowsill. Zach stood in front of Den in his armchair.

She nodded at Tom by way of a greeting. "Oh God." Emotion swelled inside her at the state of Den. "The poor man."

"Awful, isn't it," Zach said. "Going by the temperature reading I took, he's been dead around three hours, so about fiveish."

Helena glanced at the cuckoo clock on the wall. The little doors on the front were open, and the cuckoo glared out at her from inside his cubby hole as if annoyed he couldn't push them outwards and make a grand entrance on the chime of the hour.

It was eight-fifty now. Another ten minutes, and the bird would pop out.

"Right." She didn't know what else to say. Seeing Den like this seemed to have erased all her police training. She told herself to pretend it wasn't him, and her mind kicked into gear. "What about his son?"

"I did a quick ear temp before coming up here, and he's a lot later. About eight?"

The idea that they'd turned up so soon after the killer had left chilled her.

"So he possibly arrived here, caught the killer with Den, and got murdered himself—a witness that needed to be eliminated?" She was talking to herself really, not expecting an answer. It helped to get the words out into the open.

"I've lived here all my bloody life," Andy said, moving closer to stand beside her, "and I've known Mark ever since I can remember, his dad, too. I can't think of anyone who'd want to do this to them. It beggars belief."

"Me neither," Zach said. "One of the kindest men I know. It seems bloody rotten that I'll be doing a PM on a man who used to ruffle my hair when I was a kid."

"Same." Andy blinked a fair few times.

"Crikey." Helena let out a long sigh. The image of Den being kind to Zach and Andy when they were little brought on misty eyes syndrome.

"Note the difference?" Zach asked.

Helena tried to get her mind into the now. "What do you mean?"

"Several stab wounds, same as his son, but minimal blood surrounding the chair compared to downstairs."

"Yes, I'd noted that with the son but hadn't registered it here. Sorry, I'm not firing on all cylinders at the minute."

She mentally kicked herself and studied the scene. The blood stopped at the chair arm edges, and only a few drops had dripped onto the floor either side. Castoff had arced up the wall behind Den, on the ceiling, streaking that clock, and a puddle of red sat at his feet, but really, for the level of rage used in the attack, there wasn't enough blood.

"Same as at Felicity's," she said.

"Makes me wonder whether he erected some sort of tent," Andy said. "But not a tent, just something that stops the blood spreading."

"Why, though?" Helena pondered. "The killer's got to have been covered in blood—tent or not, if she's standing in front of Den here, she's going to get it on her. To walk out of here with that all over her is bold as fuck."

129

"If she left out the back and went down the alley, we have all those houses that'll need door-to-door enquiries carried out," Andy said. "I'll ring for that now, shall I?"

"Please," she said. "And make sure they do this street and all. Lots of shops with residents living above them. Someone must have seen or heard something."

Andy left the room, and Helena studied it.

"He didn't finish his dinner," she said, her words rising with grief.

A plate of half-eaten fish and chips sat on a tray on the coffee table.

"He was probably disturbed," Zach said. "Either a knock at the door, or whoever it was breaking in and coming up here. The son doesn't have any defensive wounds on his hands, neither does Den, so they didn't try to fight off the killer either in this room or at the bottom of the stairs—and the son was stabbed down there. No blood on the stairs—other than the first three—or the walls going down as far as I saw."

"So Den gets murdered up here, then the killer goes down and offs the son?" Helena frowned, trying to work out why the murderer had been up here and Mark wasn't. "Maybe Den was here alone, the killer came, then later, Mark turned up?"

"Possibly."

She didn't want to think of Mark tied up in the storeroom, knowing his dad was being stabbed, but she had to consider it. How awful if that had been the case.

"I'll have to check whether Mark lived here or elsewhere. He could have a wife somewhere. Clive might know." She gave him a ring and asked.

"Yes, guv. He's married; not sure what she's called, though. He's the manager of Nationwide. Got a little kid, too."

"Fuck…a kid. Do you know him well enough to have his address?"

"No, sorry."

"Can you contact the station for me and get the details? I'll need his wife's name, too."

"Okay."

She cut the call and held her phone by her side, and another rang, off in the distance somewhere.

"Victim's mobile's ringing," someone called from downstairs. "Says Natasha on the screen."

"Okay, thanks. Don't answer it," she shouted.

Her phone jangled, and she swiped the screen. "Yep."

"Natasha Simons," Clive said. "Fifty-two Welbeck Avenue."

"Cheers." She put her phone in her pocket. "That was the wife ringing him."

"Christ," Zach said. "I can't even begin to imagine having that news brought to my door."

Andy came back in. "Uniforms are on the way."

"Okay, well, as this is all so…recent, there's not much we can glean apart from it undoubtedly being the same killer, so we may as well go and see his wife."

"Not going to enjoy that," Andy said.

"Me neither, but it's got to be done. He's clearly meant to be home by now, seeing as she rang him. Best we get there quickly. She might be worrying, not that we're going to be able to alleviate that. We're just going to make it worse." Helena gave the room another once-over. Two chairs at the small dining table hadn't been pushed in properly, but that might not mean anything. A clothes airer leant against them, and that might not mean anything either, but it stuck in her mind as odd.

"Tom, can you have a quick look at those chairs for me, please?"

He left the windowsill and walked over to the small table. "Blood spots on the seats, but only on the front edges. And they're in a line, as if something was on the seats, partially covering them."

"Yet there doesn't seem to be any blood going from Den to the chairs," she said, studying the carpet.

"No." Tom moved to his bag by the door to get out a swab kit.

"The chairs must have been closer to Den, then they were put back," she said.

She returned her attention to him. He'd been hit in the face. Drying blood left two tracks from his nostrils, and his lip had been split. Zach was undoing Den's shirt, which was ripped from stab wounds, but she was unable to determine how many as the shirt was now red and dark instead of cream like the collar, which only had speckles of blood on it.

Zach peeled back the fronts, and Helena's pie asked to come back out. She clamped her teeth and tried to think of something else, but the state of Den's stomach was right there, compelling her to look at it. Some of the slices had merged into others, and parts of his innards peeped out.

"I can't," she said. "I'm going to have to go."

Zach nodded, and Andy turned away from the body, his shoulders rising as he retched.

The cuckoo sang out its two-tone tune.

Nine o'clock then.

Helena walked out without saying goodbye, worried if she unclamped her teeth, she'd be sick. She went downstairs, climbing over Mark's body, and rushed through the storeroom. Out in the fresh air, she took several gulps, ripping off her white suit and snatching off the gloves. She'd keep the booties on until they got to the

133

car. Tears stinging, she stuffed the clothing in a cardboard box beside Clive and made eye contact with him.

"Fucking horrendous, isn't it, guv," he said.

She nodded. "We're…um…we're going out the front to wait for the uniforms, then we'll be visiting Mark's wife."

"Okay," Clive said.

Helena hung around until Andy had disposed of his outfit, then they left the yard and walked down the alley. On the path outside Den's, she coached herself calm. It wouldn't do to visit Natasha Simons all distraught.

Once the uniforms arrived and she'd given them instructions, she took her booties off and got in the car.

She wasn't looking forward to the next step one bit.

CHAPTER TWELVE

Fifty-two Welbeck Avenue was a grand affair that must have cost a pretty penny. It was set at the end of a wide drive, majestic-looking with its own Victorian streetlamp to the right, spilling white light onto the asphalt and splashing on the brickwork. The lead-paned windows gave it a luxurious air, and bushes pruned to within an inch of their lives sat stoutly beneath the two front windows either side of the black front door.

Helena rang the bell, and a light flickered on next to the door, another Victorian effort, the shade black with a fleur-de-lis on top. A figure approached, the shape indistinct through the stained-glass portions of the centrepiece—red roses on winding green stems.

Red roses.

Helena shivered.

The door opened, and a woman appeared, blonde, blue-eyed, and slender, and Helena's mind zipped to the description of the lady in the street at Felicity's. This one had red jeans on and a long grey jumper that reached her knees, her feet snuggled inside cream boot slippers with satin ribbon bows on the sides.

Another woman popped her head out of a room at the end of the wide hall, an older version of Natasha Simons, and that was handy. Helena wouldn't have to ask Natasha if there was anyone they could call to sit with her once she'd broken the news.

She disliked herself for that thought.

"Hello. I'm DI Helena Stratton, and this is DS Andy Mald." She held up her ID. "It's better if we come in. You *are* Natasha Simons, yes?"

Natasha nodded. "What's going on?" She paled and stepped back to allow them entry, her hand shaking by her side, a fuck-off massive diamond ring twinkling on her finger. "This is my mum, by the way."

"Hi," the mum said, walking closer, her grey shoes shushing on the wooden flooring. "I'm Iris Banks."

Helena and Andy stepped inside, and Natasha closed the door.

"Can we go and sit somewhere?" Helena asked, casting her gaze around at the large hallway, big enough to accommodate a black two-seater sofa to the left, a white side table with flowers and greenery in a yellow vase beside it. Their scent perfumed the air, and she thought about the funerals to come and how the smell of flowers wouldn't be the same for this family anymore.

"Of course." Natasha gestured to a panelled door. "What's happened? Did Mark have an accident on the way home? My husband…"

"Best we sit down." Helena walked through the doorway into a plush living room, the sofa and chairs burnt orange, the walls cream, a white coffee table reminiscent of IKEA in front of the sofa, and a cream-and-orange geometric-patterned rug sitting in the centre on dark laminate flooring. It was all posh yet didn't have Helena feeling out of place. She hated homes where she thought if she breathed it would make a mess.

Natasha and Iris sat on the sofa, close to each other, and Iris grabbed Natasha's hand. Helena and Andy chose the chairs opposite.

"We're here about Mark and your father-in-law, Den," Helena said, looking at Natasha. "Was Mark meant to be there tonight?"

Natasha nodded. "Yes, he goes once a week, usually for eight, but he left early so he could get

137

back to watch a programme at nine. I rang him, actually, to remind him, but he didn't answer, and I got worried and thought...he'd crashed the car."

The remembered sound of Mark's phone ringing echoed in Helena's head, ghostly and sad. "I'm afraid I have some bad news. I'm sorry to say Mark and Den were fatally stabbed this evening."

Natasha blinked, and it was clear she was processing that information. Slowly. Iris gasped and slapped her free hand over her mouth, a muffled moan creeping out from behind it. With Natasha still mute, Helena took the opportunity to ask a question.

"Do you know of anyone who would have wanted to do that to them?"

Her words just hung there, tension buzzing.

Natasha's eyes overspilled. She shook her head. "Mark's...*dead*?"

Iris lowered her hand and rubbed her chest. "Why? Why would anyone do this?"

"We don't know," Helena said. "And, yes, they're both dead." God, that had come out so blunt. But how could she soften something like that? To coat it with icing and put a cherry on top wasn't going to help matters. "Early indications show that Den was stabbed first, and Mark had perhaps arrived and disturbed the killer." She winced — it was so difficult to say these things to people, knowing their hearts were breaking, their minds full of terrible images, but she had to. "It's so important for us to know if there were any grudges, any reason why anyone would want to hurt them."

Natasha stared blankly. "No, I can't think..." She turned to her mother. "There's no one, is there?"

"No, not that I'm aware of," Iris said. "They're both lovely men. I've known Den all my life, and he's never had a bad word to say about anyone. Not to me anyway. And as for Mark, he's cut from the same cloth. He's a gentleman, a kind person." Her eyebrows shot up. "Would this have anything to do with the building society, do you think?"

"It's something we'll be looking into, certainly, but that doesn't explain why the person we're searching for would be at Den's." Unless it was to use him as bait to lure Mark to the shop, but then what about Felicity? Or weren't the crimes connected at all, and it was just a coincidence they'd all been stabbed several times? Helena glanced at Andy and moved her eyes to give him the signal to make some tea. "Perhaps Den upset someone in the shop, a customer maybe."

Andy got up and left the room.

Iris frowned. "I just can't see it."

"Oh God. Lizzie..." Natasha stared at the rug.

Helena raised her eyebrows at Iris, silently asking who that was.

"My granddaughter," Iris said. "She's one next week. Mark had organised such a lovely day for her…"

Bloody hell… "I'm so sorry." She was, too. A little girl was going to grow up without her daddy, his loss felt for years to come. She took a deep breath. All this emotion was a tad overwhelming for her, so God only knew what Natasha and Iris were feeling. "Andy is just making you some tea, then I have some more questions. I realise it's difficult to answer them at a time like this, but we need to ask them in order to find who did this as quickly as possible." *Before they target someone else.*

Both women nodded, Iris rubbing Natasha's back, and Natasha gazed vacantly ahead, her forehead ruffled. Helena guessed she was in shock. Grief would pour out soon—it could be in the following minute, tomorrow, or next week, but it would come, drowning her with its cruel severity.

They sat in silence until Andy returned with two cups, white with big orange flowers on the sides, a yellow dot in the centre. He placed them on wooden coasters on the coffee table then retook his seat, clearing his throat as if that would rid the air of the horrible taint of death's aftermath.

"We have reason to believe these murders are connected to another one," Helena began. "A woman named Felicity Greaves was also stabbed in her home, and there are similarities I can't divulge at present that have cemented the belief they're linked. Do you know her?"

A flicker of something swept across Natasha's face. Was she entertaining a memory? "From school. She was in the year below me. I don't know her in any way other than that."

"I knew her mother," Iris said. "Also school related, but I said hello every so often when we were older, if we bumped into each other in shops or whatever. I doubt this is relevant, but she topped herself after her fella got killed in an accident. He got crushed in his lorry. I remember Felicity went to live with her gran, Gladys someone or other."

"Okay." Helena had a think about how to word her next query and also how to reveal it was a female they were searching for. She decided to just say it outright. "So if we think about Felicity, Mark, and Den, is there any person linking them together? I'm talking a woman here."

Natasha snapped out of her funk at that, her cheeks turning pink, her mouth forming a thin, tight line, as though anger had her in its grip. "A woman? Mark wouldn't have…he would never have cheated. You can't be telling me that." Her

141

bottom lip wobbled, and fresh tears rolled out the red carpet, waiting for grief to step on it and become the star of the show.

"That's not what I'm thinking at all," Helena said gently, annoyed she hadn't put it better. "The lady we're after has blonde hair, long, and was outside Felicity's on the night of her murder. It's very difficult, I know, to imagine a woman doing this, but we have a witness, and we have to follow that line of enquiry."

Iris swallowed, crying herself now. "If you think Mark arrived there and disturbed the killer, taking him completely out of the equation, and we only think about a woman wanting to kill Felicity and Den, it doesn't make sense. She's young, and Den's old. What could possibly link them?"

That had crossed Helena's mind and was confusing her, too. They weren't related, they were poles apart in lifestyle, and nothing about their connection added up. "This is what we're desperate to find out. Any link, however slim, would be of help."

"I can't think of anything," Natasha said. "We don't really socialise these days. Mark and I go to the pub maybe once every three months or so—Mum looks after Lizzie—but we don't meet up with friends or anything." Her voice was low and weak, hard to hear. "Mark's busy at work, so when he comes home he just wants to relax, and I don't particularly keep in touch with anyone. I'm too busy with Lizzie. The days just merge into one another." She pulled her hand from her mother's and wiped her cheeks. "I-I'm sorry, but this is all a bit too much. I want to scream...to run and..."

Thinking it best to leave them be for now, Helena got up. "I understand. Thank you for your time, and I'm sorry for your loss. Someone will be in contact about formal identification and when the bodies will be released. If you feel you need to speak to a family liaison officer, Dave Lund is a lovely man who can help you with many things. Would you like him to call round tomorrow?"

Natasha nodded. "I-I think so. I have no idea what to do..."

Iris stood at the same time as Andy.

"I won't be a minute, love." She patted Natasha's shoulder. "I'll see you out," she said to Helena.

At the open front door, Helena shivered at the chill wind that gusted in, and she stepped out into the rain that pelted down so hard it bounced off the drive. She smiled at Iris and handed her a card that had various numbers on it as well as Dave's. Then she offered her own.

"Give him a ring first thing," Helena said, "so he can come straight out. Tell him I gave you his card. I'll send him an email in a second as well.

If you or Natasha think of anything, call me, all right? Take care now." She turned and made a dash for the car, clicking the key fob to get the doors unlocked.

In the driver's seat, damp and dogged off at the weather, she used her phone to send Dave's email, then, with Andy beside her, reversed out of the drive and into the street.

"We'll need to nip to the station to do a check on CCTV and social media, just a quick look in case it gives us something we can use tonight." She glanced at the clock on the dash. "We'll give it until midnight, yes?"

"Yep."

"I don't bloody get this at all," she said, straining to see through the windscreen. Even though the wipers were on, the deluge was excessive. Wind rocked the car, and she gripped the steering wheel in an attempt to keep the vehicle from slewing to the side. "I mean, they're connected but not. Make sense?"

"Yeah. Connected by death, but what the hell else it is, I have no idea. One person clearly had a beef with them, but I can't figure out what it might be. Maybe Facebook and the like will offer us some insight, but can you see Den being on it?"

"Not really, not unless he has a business page. Christ, this weather is nasty. Look at that gutter over there."

Water churned against the kerb, rushing towards the drain. Trees either side of the road bent over slightly, their bare branches wavering as if to ward Mother Nature off. Rain came sideways, smacking into Helena's window, the slap of it loud and unsettling.

"Bloody global warming," Andy said, folding his arms across his chest.

"And to think some people don't believe it exists."

She pulled into the station car park, and they ran inside, cold rain soaking Helena's hair in seconds. Inside, she trudged up the stairs and walked through to her office, draping her coat over the back of the desk chair, grabbed a spare T-shirt she kept in the cupboard, and dried off her hair with a small towel.

She joined Andy in the incident room. He was already on the phone to CCTV, so Helena sat at Ol's desk and booted up the computer. Accessing Facebook, she did a search for Den and, finding nothing whatsoever, she checked for Mark. His page was public, so she could nose at anything and everything. Pictures of him, Natasha, and baby Lizzie were predominant, as were some of a holiday to the Algarve last year, Lizzie in an adorable little sun hat, her cheeks pink, one bottom tooth sticking up in an otherwise gummy smile, her dress spilling out over her legs while she sat on the sand. It was all

145

so perfect, so lovely, and Helena imagined Natasha looking at those photos in the future and crying over what had been and what was lost.

Checking his friend list, she found nothing regarding Felicity, which didn't surprise her. Mark had few contacts—fifty-one—and they were mainly men, perhaps mates from school or work colleagues. No one had said anything untoward on his timeline, and he didn't post or comment all that much, a meme here and there or a link to a news article.

She decided to leave the proper digging for Ol tomorrow and ask her to contact Natasha to see if she knew Mark's password, although forensics would have his phone, and if Mark logged on to any apps, he might not sign out, so they could check his Messenger and see if anything showed up there.

"Want a coffee?" she asked, rising and moving towards the vending machine.

"A hot chocolate if there are any, although I'll be surprised if there are."

She popped some coins into the slot and selected Andy's drink. "Prepare to be surprised." A cup winged its way out onto the silver grate and filled with hot chocolate. "I'm going to have one and all." She handed him his, then pressed the button again. "And, just like that, fate's being a bastard. Coffee it is for me then."

"Ah, the CCTV files are here," Andy said.

Helena placed her cup on his desk and scooted Ol's chair over. She briefly wondered how Phil had fared at dinner with Yarworth and hoped he'd picked a good candidate to join their team.

Sitting beside Andy, she waited while he accessed the CCTV in Den's street.

At seven-forty, Mark parked, got out, and disappeared down the alley. She shivered at that being the last time anyone other than the killer, or perhaps Den, had seen him alive. A few cars drove by, and Helena wrote down the number plates, but no one walked along the street. After eight, Clive drew up and got out.

"Is that it? Just the file at the front of the shop?" she asked.

"There's another. Let's see what it is." Andy minimised the window and clicked on the second file. "I'll just scoot along on fast-forward until we get to what, six o'clock?"

"That'll do," she said, then sipped her coffee, scalding her bloody tongue.

With the time reached, Andy set it to slow-forward. It was the scene of the back of the shops, darkness shrouding everything except for a lamppost bursting with light at the end of the alley. The camera must be mounted a few shops along from Den's, and it pointed to the left, showing the bottom of Den's yard and a partial of the alleyway.

"Go forward a bit faster to around ten to eight, when we know Mark was there," she said.

Andy did, and they watched it at normal speed for a while, then someone appeared, walking down the alley to the right of the screen.

"Stop," she said. Eight-fifteen. "Now, no one entered that alley from the front, so they had to have come from Den's or the ice cream shop beside it." She peered at the screen. "Woman my fucking arse."

"That's what I thought."

The screen was paused on the image of a man, a roll of something or other balanced on his shoulder, a backpack in his hand. The colour of his top wasn't discernible on the black-and-white footage, but it was a dark one. His hair, short and clipped, was also dark.

"Are we looking at two people here?" Andy asked. "A woman for Felicity, a man for Den and Mark?"

"Fuck knows, but our job has just got a whole lot more interesting."

CHAPTER THIRTEEN

*O*n the last day ever of secondary school, at the end of the day, he stared at Mark across the playground. Mark had been iffy with him lately, as though something was up. What was it, though?

Fucked if I know.

He scuffed his shoe on the asphalt, displacing a few errant stones, and told himself to just go over there and ask. But what if Mark told him to knob off? He wasn't sure what he'd do if he did. Mark was the only proper friend he had, so getting into anything with him on the argument front wasn't something he thought he could hack.

"Fuck it," he muttered and made his way over.

Everyone milled about, showing off their spare uniform shirts signed by people they liked and some they didn't. Black marker pens had sold out in

Rymans because of all the year elevens buying them, which meant he'd had to make do with a dumb blue biro. Not that anyone had asked him to sign their shirt. He'd basically had to force himself on them, make them let him. All he wanted was to belong, to be as important as the other kids, but it seemed Eddie was right: You're nothing, kid. Nothing at all.

Well, he'd show Eddie. He'd be somebody one day, just you wait and bloody see.

He got closer to Mark, and someone jostled him, that Benny kid, almost sending him flying onto his arse. Annoyed, he shoved Benny in the back as he walked off with his friend, and Benny sprawled onto the playground, signed shirt floating off, hands splayed flat on the tarmac.

"Stupid prick," he said.

Benny looked over his shoulder then turned away, pushing himself to his feet. Ready for a fight, was he? No. Benny strolled on, head bent, his mate scooping up the shirt and chasing after him.

Enough was enough, wasn't it? He didn't have to take crap from any of these wankers anymore. He wasn't a schoolboy now, he was on his way to becoming a bloke, and once he was, everyone had better watch the fuck out.

They'd soon see not to mess with him.

Mark glanced down, like he didn't want anything to do with the incident — or him. What was his problem?

Ask him outright, go on.

"Look, man, what's the deal?" he asked.

Mark moved away from the lads standing around him, jerking his head to indicate they should be alone. "I can't hang around with you, that's what."

Frowning, he didn't know what to say. What could *he* say except, "Why?"

"Dad says you're a bad influence – or you're going to be." Mark shrugged, his cheeks going a tad red.

That bloody Den…

"I don't get it," he said, eyeing Mark for signs of him caving, for him to smile and say he'd only been pissing about. "What have I done for your old man to think that?" *Apart from all the little jobs he'd been doing for Eddie… Had Den found out? Had Eddie bragged about it in the pub or something?*

"Don't know," Mark said, "but I'd better do as he says. I'm going to college then uni. I can't have my future fucked up."

"But I won't fuck it up. You're my mate. Why would I do that?"

"Look, sod off, will you? This is hard enough as it is."

"So I'm meant to just accept it, is that what you're saying?"

"Something like that. We're going in different directions. We…"

He tuned him out. Those were Den's words floating out of Mark's mouth. *What had happened to their pact about always sticking together? What about buddies for life, eh?*

"Don't do this," he said, waiting for Mark to start laughing, anything to show this wasn't real.

He didn't.

"I can't go against my dad," Mark said. "We've had a proper chat, and it's important I don't mess my life up."

"Come on, change your mind." He hated the way he sounded all pleading and shit.

"No."

Mark scowled at him then ran off.

Mark had said no.

God. He was going to have to pay for that.

Words echoed in his head, Eddie gassing on about bad things happening. The thing was, he didn't know what the bad things were.

He'd ask Eddie.

On the way home, he dumped his shirt in a bin, wanting nothing to do with any of the people who'd scribbled their names on it, no visual memories. He had enough of them in his head, and seeing the shirt would just rile him up.

At home, he found Mum passed out drunk on the sofa, her mouth open, spittle dripping over her chin. Litter was dotted all around – they'd forgotten what a bloody bin was for. He sighed and went to the kitchen, getting a black bag out of the cupboard under the sink. He cleaned up, shoving beer cans, crisp packets, and small Bacardi bottles in it, disgusted by the pigsty this place had become. He vaguely remembered it being tidy once, and clean, when Dad was here and before the drink and Eddie had tumbled onto the scene.

He wouldn't mind if he got a bit of pocket money for being the maid, but it seemed it was his job now. Talking of jobs, he had another one to do later for Eddie, although he'd yet to find out what it was.

Some said if you talked about the Devil he'd appear, and there he was, Eddie, walking down the stairs in nothing but brown checked pyjama bottoms, scratching his crotch. He hadn't shaved for ages, and an unkempt beard had sprouted, some hairs longer than others.

"All right, you little fucker?" Eddie asked, walking past and into the kitchen. As usual, he hadn't noticed the mess had been binned.

Anger burned inside. He followed Eddie and shut the kitchen door. "You know you said bad things happen if people say no? What are they? The bad things, I mean."

Eddie sneered. "If you say no, I'll kill you. That plain enough?"

Christ.

To show the answer didn't faze him, even though it bleedin' well did, he said, "What's today's job?" He opened the back door and tossed the rubbish bag out, then closed it and turned the taps on ready for doing the washing up. He couldn't let Eddie know he'd scared him with what he'd said — Eddie would use it against him.

"Den's again." Eddie lit a ciggie then switched the kettle on.

"I can't," he said. "Mark's told me we're not allowed to be mates anymore. Den said I'm trouble."

"Well, he's not wrong there, is he." Eddie chuckled and held his hand out for a clean cup.

Teeth gritted, he washed it and passed it over.

Eddie didn't bother wiping the bubbles off with a tea towel. He plonked a teabag inside. "You could still go. It's summer. His place will be packed. Do what you always do and scoot into the storeroom."

"I don't think he'll even want me in the shop." He scrubbed at a plate, thick with sauce from last night's dinner, a stew he'd made that Mum hadn't eaten, preferring to stick to her liquid diet. "What about somewhere else?"

"No, got to be Den's. I have people waiting on the fags. They've already paid me. Do it just once more, then I'll think of someplace else."

It was on the tip of his tongue to say no, but he knew what Eddie would say to that. What he always did. And now he knew what the bad thing was, he wasn't about to argue.

"All right. I'll go now."

He left the plates to soak and walked out, heading for Den's, thinking Eddie had better hurry up in getting dressed if he was going to make it round the back of Den's yard in time to collect the goods.

Mark had told him someone kept stealing cigarettes and that Den would be putting 'measures' in place, whatever the fuck they were. He didn't care so long as he could get it over and done with.

He walked past Den's and, as predicted, it teemed with people. Inside the shop, he did what he always

154

did and crouched amongst the shoppers, then made his way to the storeroom.

The door was locked.

So that was what Den had decided on, was it?

He left the shop and thought about what to do next. He pinned his sights on the shop a few doors down that sold all manner of junk, an idea coming to mind. A good one, if he played it right.

Strolling in, he mingled with the holidaymakers, reaching out for a plastic mask, an old witch one with straggly grey hair and a wart on the end of her nose. He stuffed it under his top along with a black toy gun, then acted like he was browsing, instead checking he wasn't being watched.

Back outside, he waited down the alley. An hour passed with him mapping out how he'd do what he had to do, and his phone beeped with a message: Where are you?

Christ, he'd forgotten Eddie would have been out the back all this time.

He replied: I'm down the alley. Waiting for everyone to leave. Storeroom locked.

Eddie's reply was swift: Fuck.

Shrugging, he slid the mask on, and something happened. He felt different. Stronger. Better.

He could get used to this.

He put the gun in his pocket and peered around the edge of the building. Den was talking to some woman and her two kids outside, all decked out in summer gear, the late-afternoon sun beaming down on the children's red baseball caps. Their mum waved and walked off, and Den went inside, the door slowly sailing closed. Den never shut it in the summer, jamming a wedge beneath it to keep it open, so now was the time to act – Den was obviously ready to lock up.

He raced along, slammed his palms on the door, and pushed it inwards as Den moved to twist the key. Holding the gun up, he waggled it about, thinking it looked well menacing, and advanced on a retreating Den whose face was a bloody picture. Terrified, he was. What a gimp.

"Open the storeroom," he said, all growly, sounding nothing like himself and loving it.

Den raised one hand and with the other pulled a bunch of keys out of his pocket. Why wasn't he shouting for Mrs Simons or Mark, the stupid bastard?

Den unlocked the door and shoved it open.

Gun steady, he jabbed it towards him and said, "Get in there."

Den obeyed.

Taking his chance, he whacked the old boy on the temple with his elbow, sending him sprawling into a stack of boxes. One came down and smacked him on the head, and it had to have hurt, because the wording on the side said: JACOB'S JAR SWEETS.

Ouch then.

He held back a laugh at Den out cold on the floor, his face partially hidden by the box, and snatched the keys out of Den's limp grasp. He opened the back door and lobbed out boxes of cigarettes until there *were none left. That'd serve Den right for trying to stop him from nicking them.*

Outside, he made trips back and forth across the yard, tossing the boxes over the wall, then climbing it and landing on the other side to help Eddie put them in the van. Eddie stared at him as though he'd seen a damn ghost – the mask had obviously thrown him for a second.

He climbed inside the back and closed the doors, and Eddie got in the front and sped away through the streets of the estate where no one told anyone anything and everyone kept their mouths shut. Sweat covered his face, and he wrenched the mask off, instantly feeling like his old self again. Unwanted. Unimportant.

The next day, it was on the local radio that Den had been assaulted and robbed. The police were on the lookout for whoever had done it, and the woman who'd been talking to Den with her kids had turned around to glance back over her shoulder and spotted an old lady entering the shop, her grey hair long and straggly, her clothes similar to a school uniform.

Old lady. He laughed at that.

Masks would come in handy for future jobs, even though he'd never been caught for anything before when he hadn't had one on, which just went to show how well Eddie had trained him.

So I'm good for something then.

157

He was good for something all right. Killing and making people realise if they said no, he'd make sure the bad thing happened. Who had they thought they were, treating him the way they had?

It was past midnight, and he couldn't get to sleep. His mojo was off. Mark being there earlier had tossed him into a whirlpool of doubt, although in the end, a deviation in the plan hadn't completely put him off his stride. He'd dealt with the new occurrence swiftly, and it had made the local news at ten on the telly, the bloke behind the desk on the screen saying a policeman close to the source had said the three murders were abhorrent and the killer would be caught quickly.

Dream on.

He'd resisted going back to the scene. He imagined, once the coppers had turned up, that all those nosy bastards living in the flats above the shops would have come out to see what was going on. They'd have been questioned, no doubt, but no one would have seen him. The alley was too dark, and as for those on the estate out the back, folks there tended to mind their own business, just like they had when he'd been a kid.

That was handy.

He thought about the bitch he was going to murder next. She had plans to be at The

Villager's Inn on a hen night. He'd heard about it the other week while having a bevvy in there. She'd be pissed up, her brain a bit fuddled, and that was a good thing.

Either way, she'd better enjoy the evening, because it was going to be her last.

CHAPTER FOURTEEN

Sleep had been interrupted with bad dreams. Helena had stared at the ceiling in the dark, willing morning to come. The last thing she'd wanted was to visit the gym before work, but she'd told Andy she'd help to get him in shape, and that was what she'd do. He'd made sure to run at a slower speed on the treadmill this time, so there were no mishaps for her to laugh at, and they'd made it to the station by eight to begin work.

Ol and Phil had been shocked at waltzing in thinking they'd only have Felicity's murder to deal with. The looks on their faces when Helena had told them about Den and Mark had been a picture.

With all the information related to them, she set them to it, then walked over to Phil. "How did it go last night?" she asked.

He put his pen down and turned to face her. "Bloody excruciating."

"What do you mean?" She crouched beside his chair.

"Yarworth went on about the Walker case as if he'd solved the bleeding thing himself. I mean, it's not like us four worked our bollocks off or anything, is it." He shook his head and huffed out a breath of exasperation. "It boiled my piss, to be honest. I was watching everyone else while he was talking, and they seemed to think he was a bit of a dick. Let's face it, he sits in that office all day doing sod all, then has a quick read of the files once we're done and signs them off."

"Better than him being in our faces, believe me," she said. "Can you imagine working closely with him?"

"No, I don't want to even think about it." He gave an exaggerated shudder.

Helena laughed. "You and me both. So, what about the people who want new jobs? What were they like?"

"They were all nice enough, but the one who stuck out for me was a bloke called Evan. He knows what he's about, and I think he'll be a good fit. He mentioned to me he thought

162

Yarworth was an 'up his own arse prat', so that sealed it."

"Did you tell Yarworth Evan would be right for us?"

"Yeah. He'll be joining us next month. He's wanting to finish helping out on a case in Essex first, which tells me he's as dedicated as we are."

"Brilliant. Learn anything about him?"

"He's married, got two small kids, one of each. Think he said they're five and seven. His wife's a teacher, so she'll be starting at Smaltern Primary. Year two, I'm sure he said."

"Sounds great. Thanks for going. And it was a good job you did, really, what with Mark and Den."

"I'm shocked," he said. "My brother went to school with Mark, and he's a good sort. And Den's like everyone's grandad, know what I mean?"

"Yep. It wasn't pleasant to see, I have to say. Right, I'll leave you be."

The day passed with everyone poking into the victims' backgrounds and ringing their friends and family. Helena thought about visiting Natasha Simons again but decided to phone the FLO, Dave Lund, instead.

She went into her office about half four to do it. "You still there?"

"No, I stayed for most the morning and talked through all that will happen next. She's

163

formally identifying the day after tomorrow as Zach is still working on them—I rang him to check. All she told me was that Mark and Den were lovely people and she had absolutely no idea why anyone would do this."

"Same as what she told me," she said, "which doesn't help us at all. Anyway, thanks for that. I'll give Zach a bell now."

She did, and it rang for ages. She assumed he was elbow deep in blood and guts and was about to hang up when he answered.

"Hey, you," he said. "I just had to get the gloves off and wash my hands."

"Nice. I'm ringing about work. I know I shouldn't bug you when you haven't sent any findings back yet, but we've had a frustrating day checking into things and getting nothing except how nice Mark and Den were. No one saw anything in the shop street, and those in the estate out the back haven't given us anything to work with either. We're stuck."

"Well, it's the same killer as far as I can tell," Zach said. "The knife wounds resemble those of Felicity, and with both Mark and Den, there are twenty-three."

"That's just bloody creepy," she said. "Someone's counting them as they stab? No way that can be a coincidence."

"I thought the same. And they'd have to be controlled if they can attack so violently and not lose count. Scary really."

"Too right. We found out something interesting last night which flushes your theory down the shitter."

"What's that then?"

"It might be two killers."

"Ah, but they'd have to be using the same type of knife, which is a stretch of the imagination. So how did you discover that?"

"Good old CCTV. There's a camera installed on the back of one of the shops. A male walked down the alley at the right time carrying a roll of something and a backpack. No one else went down there before or after, so it can only be the person we're looking for."

"Man and woman team?" he asked.

"Maybe. Could be a couple with a shared grudge. The thing is, that's a lot of trust. They've got to be totally sure of each other to be doing this." She paused to think. "Or one of them is forcing the other to do it, and that could get messy later on down the line if the unwilling party decides to say something to a mate. Anyway, I've wandered off course. Do you have anything else?"

"Den's stomach contents contained a small amount of undigested fish and chips, so he hadn't had much time to eat before the killer arrived. Say he ate about five o'clock, that means the killer hung around for a while afterwards if the food was still in Den's stomach."

"Hmm, the suspect was in the alley at eight-fifteen, so he left near enough straight after killing Mark. Why would he want to hang around after stabbing Den? Unless he knew Mark was due... So it could be someone who knows people's movements."

"I assume so, but that's your side of things."

"What about Mark's stomach?"

"His food was also undigested, and at a guess — I won't know until it's analysed — he had pasta and minced beef. I see so many types of food during PMs that I'm beginning to recognise the meals. Good job it doesn't put me off my dinner really."

She closed her eyes as an image of spaghetti Bolognese entered her head. "God. It's so bloody awful. He ate that not knowing it was his last meal."

"Unless we're talking being told we're going to die at a certain time, none of us know. That's why it's always best to have a pudding."

She opened her eyes and smiled. "Except we missed out on our dessert last night." Crap, she wondered whether that had come off as an innuendo so gabbled on, "I quite fancied the apple crumble and custard myself."

He chuckled. "And there was me thinking you meant something else entirely."

Oh bugger. How to respond? "Um, maybe next time." That was all right, wasn't it? Not too forward?

"I'm joking. I won't push you into anything. Not after…" He cleared his throat.

No, not after Uthway and his bully boy had violated her, but she had to impress upon him how things were with her now. "Oh, I'm fine. I can differentiate, thankfully, and I'm lucky I can. Some people…" She blushed. "I mean, I don't associate…"

"I know what you're saying. Whenever you're ready. It's still early days yet. I don't make a habit of, you know, doing *that* straight away. It'd be nice to get to know each other better first."

"I don't jump into bed with people either, and yes, it'll be nice to take it slow." She'd told herself when she'd ended it with Marshall that she wouldn't see anyone else for a long time, but then Zach had made it clear he liked her, and she'd liked him for so long that being with him didn't feel wrong. "If there's nothing else…"

"Only that if you're not too busy, I'd like you to come to mine for dinner tonight. You can have apple crumble, although it'll be Waitrose's finest, and I'll pour some Ambrosia on top. If I

167

try to make the custard from scratch, it'll turn out lumpy. I'm crap at cooking."

"What time?" The day had been a bust, so none of her team would be working late. They'd look at it with fresh eyes tomorrow. Maybe something would jump out at them then, but she doubted it.

"Seven? I'm about to wrap up here. I finished Felicity's PM and did partials on Mark and Den, so I'll complete theirs tomorrow."

"Okay, I just have one more person to ring, then I'm calling it a day myself. See you later."

She rang Tom in forensics.

"All right, guv?" he said, chipper, a laugh lingering in his voice, as though there'd been some joke or other going on before he'd answered.

"Yes, you?"

"Fine, thanks. What can I do for you?"

"Has anyone had a chance to look at Mark's phone today?"

"As a matter of fact, I did it and was about to send you a report. No suspicious calls in or out. In the past three months they've mainly been to Den or his wife and a couple of work colleagues. No weird messages. Facebook and Messenger were logged in, and again, nothing dodgy. Just your average man's phone log, I'm afraid. I've got the messages and whatnot saved in a file for you, so I'll send it your way. I've sent the phone off for further analysis with digital forensics."

"Okay, thanks. Ol can go through your file tomorrow — not saying you need your work checked or anything."

"Nope, always best to have another set of eyes. A few of us went through the photos as well from the three death locations. Blood spatter is consistent with a right-handed person — think I mentioned that before regarding Felicity. And as I said then, we'd be able to determine height, and that's been aided with Mark's scene especially. We estimate around five-ten, although if the woman has heels on, that will make a difference."

"Not sure it's just a woman now," she said and explained what they'd discovered.

"Well, if it's two people, then they're exactly the same height, we're positive about that."

Helena had a headache coming on. There was so much information, yet at the same time, no definite clues. There had to be hundreds of people in Smaltern that tall, so it narrowed absolutely fuck all down. Typical and par for the course.

"Anything else?" She rubbed her brow, trying to ease the sudden pounding.

"Yes, and this is just as weird as the Walker case. I did wonder whether news leaking out about the gifts being left behind had given this killer some ideas."

She was annoyed about the leak. Someone from the department had tipped off a journalist, specifically mentioning the taunting clues the killer had planted.

Her stomach clenched. "Oh God, what…?"

"We didn't notice it before because there was so much blood, but at every scene, there's a little picture that's been drawn on the wall."

"What sort of picture?"

"A witch."

"Pardon?"

"Yep, a wart on its nose and everything. The only thing it doesn't have is a pointed hat. Have you watched *Snow White*?"

She nodded then remembered he wouldn't have seen her doing it. "Yes."

"Like the witch in that."

Helena frowned. "I wonder what that's supposed to mean?"

"Your guess is as good as mine, but it was done in pencil, not that it helps any."

"Were the drawings any good?"

"No, they're like a kid would draw or someone who isn't too hot at art. You can see what the images are, just that they're no Monet. There's also the number twenty-three written above the witches."

"That matches the amount of stabs each victim had. Christ." Who the hell were they dealing with?

"There are some right nutters out there. I'll send those pictures over as well so you can see."

"Thanks."

After saying their goodbyes, she put the phone on her desk and pondered what he'd told her. A witch? She accessed her emails so she could get Tom's as soon as it came in. It took about five minutes of waiting, which seemed endless and was bloody frustrating, then she saved the files and set them to print. Once they'd slid out into the tray, she got up and had a look. She skimmed through the typed data first, which confirmed what Tom had said, then she stared at the witch images.

Tom had sent two lots. One set showed them on the walls at the locations. He'd drawn a red circle around them to show just how small they were. He'd also blown them up. They were almost identical, save for a bigger nose in one and a wonky eye in another. Given their actual size, it was no wonder they hadn't been spotted until a closer inspection had been carried out on the photos. They were no bigger than a penny.

She took them into the incident room and pinned one of the larger ones up on the whiteboard.

"Guys, we've got a right weirdo on our hands." She pointed to the witch. "This was drawn on the walls. What do you make of that?"

"Bloody hell," Phil blurted. "What would that even mean?"

Ol squinted at the picture. "That they're an actual witch? That someone in their life is a witch? God knows."

"It's something to think about. Ol, you can have a look into witches tomorrow, see if there's anything significant. A bit like the Uthway case and those carved symbols. The witch itself may not be what's important." Helena tapped the whiteboard. "Tom wondered whether the killer is copying the Walker case and leaving these behind as clues, although they're not telling us much at all." She went on to tell them what Zach and Tom had said. "So, if it's two killers, they're the same height and have identical knives — bit of a stretch?"

"Maybe the lady in the street has nothing to do with this," Andy said. "She may well have tried Felicity's front door, then went off when she couldn't get in. An opportunist thief. Someone else could have come along straight after and killed Felicity — the man."

"That doesn't sound plausible either, but if there are two people, we still need to find the woman regardless. If she's going about trying to get into houses, she needs to be stopped.

However, our main priority is the killer, so I'll give Louise a ring in a minute and let her know to pass it on to uniform that a woman may be breaking and entering." Her headache throbbed. "Look, it's getting on, and we're all tired. We have nothing really so far apart from a fucking witch, so shut down and go home. We'll begin all over again tomorrow."

Helena set her alarm on her phone to wake her so she'd have time for a quick shower before going to Zach's. She needed a power nap, and it might get rid of her banging migraine, something ibuprofen had failed to do. She closed her eyes, that damn witch image looming in her mind, and wished she could shut work off once she stepped foot inside her house. She couldn't, not unless she had company, so the sooner she went to Zach's, the better.

Sleep came, and God, she sank into it more than willingly.

The driver stopped the van and climbed in the back. Helena was ready for him, standing, feet planted apart. He stared at her and laughed, then aimed a gun at her. She glared back, gauging whether

she could scoot past him and out before he had time to turn around and shoot her.

He stepped forward so fast and punched her in the face she had no time to react. Down she went, her tailbone smacking onto the floor, and she scrabbled to get upright, but he moved towards her and bent over, ripping her clothes off while she tried to fight him. He grabbed her wrists with one meaty hand. She kicked out, missing hitting him completely, incensed that she was naked and vulnerable. With his free hand, he brought something close to her arm. She didn't glance in that direction, instead looking up at him, trying to work out what he was thinking. His poker face was professional, giving nothing away, so she glanced to the side.

A sharp pain, then she registered a syringe, the needle sliding into her muscle. An almost instant lethargy overtook her, and while she sat there dumbly, he secured her wrists with rope in front of her, then tied on a blindfold.

Hauled to her feet, she stumbled as he dragged her, terrified at not being able to see and how quickly her body seemed to be sinking into nothingness. He lifted her, slinging her over his shoulder. The sea, it whooshed, and gulls let out piercing cries, and there was the sound of crunching gravel followed by the shush of feet on grass.

A creak, a whine, and she imagined a door had opened. She had no energy to hit his back or kick his legs, hanging limply as she was, her mind growing sluggish.

He grunted, and she sensed they were moving skywards, perhaps up some steps. The clank of his feet on what might be metal filtered into her foggy brain. That creak rang out again, and he walked a few paces, then she was thrown down, the surface hard on her outer thigh and hip, bits of grit digging into her skin.

She wanted to ask where she was, why she'd been brought here, but he wouldn't have answered — not if he was one of Uthway's men. He'd have been told to take her wherever and keep an eye on her. Especially with her being a copper.

He kicked her in the side, and she couldn't even scream in protest. All that emerged was a low groan, and he laughed, long and hard. It sent her nerves skittering, and she shivered, her teeth chattering.

"If you think that's bad, bitch, you just wait and see what comes next." His accent was from down south — he was a Londoner, perhaps.

Her stomach muscles spasmed, bringing on nausea, and she thought she might be sick. "I... What... Help..." God, she sounded such a useless moron. Annoyance surged through her, but she couldn't do anything with it. She was pissed off with herself for even going to Lime Street alone, like she thought she could take them on and arrest them all.

Stupid, stupid cow.

"Be quiet," he said. "You're boring me."

She sensed him come closer and held her breath. He grabbed her beneath her armpits and scooted her backwards, more grit scratching her bum and the backs of her thighs, then he let her go. Four footsteps echoed, and she guessed he'd walked away, maybe to her right. The air seemed thicker there somehow, like he was so close the heat from him touched her.

Hands pushed on her chest, and she fell backwards, her body as heavy as her mind, and cold walls pressed onto her arms, as though she sat in a corner. She managed to heft her knees up, and she would have hugged them if her body responded to the demand, but it didn't, so she just flopped.

"The boss'll be here in a minute. Best you think about what you're going to say to him. He's not happy you were spying."

She had no doubt he meant Uthway, and seeing him again wouldn't be pleasant, not now the tables had turned. It wouldn't be her interviewing him with arrogance this time but him doing it to her. She'd had him in for questioning recently, her asking him about his activities but, as she should have known, his alibis had been watertight. He wouldn't do the grunt work himself in picking up women for his business. She'd been stupid to think she could get something out of him. She should have left it, not giving him any clue they were after him.

Another stupid decision on her part.

The faint crunch of car tyres rolling over cement filtered in, and her stomach lurched. She swallowed down bile. God, there was that horrible creak again, and she knew someone else had come in. Light from the open door filtered through the blindfold, but she couldn't make anything specific out, her eyes watery and unfocused.

Footsteps clunked. One, two, three, four.
They stopped.

Silence. It seemed to stretch on forever. Breathing.
Heavy breathing. Theirs? Hers? She couldn't tell.

"So it is you." Uthway. "You daft slag pig. I
wonder…what am I going to do with you now?"

CHAPTER FIFTEEN

While he waited for the hen party to wind down, he sat in the corner of The Villager's Inn like he did most nights and thought about why he'd done what he had after he'd offed Den. He should have just left straight away and gone for Mark tonight, but something had compelled him to stay.

As he'd known it would.

The flat above the shop had been a second home of sorts, considering the amount of times he'd been there as a kid. His best memories were of having tea with Mark, Mrs Simons bustling about in the kitchen, then fussing over them at the dining table, something Mum never did. She was more than likely slumped over it than anything. He'd stayed to play until about eight on those nights, Mrs Simons worrying about him walking home alone when he'd been five or so, but he'd told her it'd be all right. Life outside in the dark wasn't a problem for him after a few years, seeing as Eddie shoved him out in the garden on the evenings when people came round to visit, buying all the stuff he'd nicked. He hadn't wanted Eddie coming to collect him from Mark's, and Eddie wouldn't anyway, even if Mrs Simons rang him to ask the dodgy wanker to do it.

He'd have most likely told her to fuck off.

"I just don't know what's got into Regina, letting that lad roam about," Mrs Simons had said to Den once, whispering in the kitchen.

Listening in the hallway, he'd pressed himself against the wall, his ears burning.

"She's turned into a right old pisshead." Den had given his usual grunt.

Den had kissed Mum on the mouth just after Dad had left. Was that a secret? He reckoned so, because once they realised he'd spotted them down by the racks of crisps in the shop on that summer holiday morning, they'd sprang apart, and Mum had gone red.

Den hadn't liked him after that.

"She doesn't care for that boy like she should," Den had continued, "and that's a wicked shame, but I still can't take to him. Sorry, but I can't help it. Maybe she feels the same way about him now. She's always been a bit harried, scatterbrained, but now she's plain strung out and off her rocker. I don't want anything to do with her. Did you hear about her in the supermarket the other day? Arguing about the price of a grape? *One* grape. Mrs Jacobs told me all about it. Said Regina made a right old fuss, and she stank of booze, swaying on her feet and all sorts."

"God, that poor child," Mrs Simons had said. "Surely there's more we can do to help."

"He has his tea here once a month, and that's enough. We're not doing any more. He's a baddun, you mark my words."

He'd hated Den in that moment.

Now he was an adult, he could understand what had happened to Mum. Dad had gone, and she'd had a few drinks to drown her sorrows, to get over the heartbreak, then the reliance on booze had taken hold, a toddy before bed turning to a small bottle. And one night, while off her tits in this very pub, Eddie had got his claws into her. Maybe she'd thought she wasn't worthy of anyone else, anyone better. Other men probably saw her for the lush she was and avoided her. Maybe she'd thought she might as well shack up with a deadbeat because all blokes would leave her in the end, so what did it matter who it was?

That was a laugh. Eddie had stuck around. And her? Well, she was dead now. She was where she belonged.

He jolted out of the far past and took his mind back to last night again. After killing Den, he'd walked around the flat, touching all the furniture, sad he couldn't feel it properly with his gloves on. Still, it reminded him of his childhood when he'd done the same thing, gliding his fingertips over a sideboard or bedside cabinet while waiting for Mark to come and find him. In later years, when hide and seek wasn't something they'd played, he'd made out he needed to visit the loo a lot, but in reality, he'd gone into other rooms instead, just so he could touch what real life was, what a proper home was.

At Den's for the last time, he'd had to caress every bit of furniture, right down to the cuckoo clock on the wall, and he'd opened the little doors and stroked the wooden bird inside. He hated that bird. When it had flung itself out at eight o'clock in his former years, it had signalled his return to his shitty world with his shitty mother and even shittier stand-in father.

Anger burned through him now, and he clutched his empty pint glass tighter. He'd only had the one, and he'd sipped it all night so far. He needed to be sharp, but if he didn't have his usual lager, someone was bound to notice.

He got up and made a point of nodding to the regulars as he left, yawning as though he was super tired and ready for his bed. People would remember that, he hoped, if they were questioned about the evening once the hen woman was found dead.

At the door, he glanced at the clock — ten-thirty. Soon chucking out time. The hens had loudly complained they all had work tomorrow, and wasn't that silly of them to have met up on a week night? Yeah, fucking stupid. They'd be leaving at eleven, so they'd said, and as far as the customers were concerned, he'd be well in his bed by then.

He walked off in the direction of home, wishing that wind would bugger off. It was nippy as anything and stung his cheeks it was that cold. Then he slipped down an alley that took him to the cliff top at the rear of her house. He'd sit in her back garden until about midnight, on the green-painted cast-iron bench she had out there. He'd already left his roll of plastic and backpack beside it.

Now all he had to do was wait.

Katy staggered out of The Villager's Inn, her legs wobbly and her mind fuzzy. Bloody hell, she'd sunk more than a few Bacardi and Cokes

183

and would regret it in the morning. Still, it wasn't every day your best mate got married, was it, and it was a couple of weeks until the wedding, so she could stay sober until then, giving her poor liver a break.

The rest of the girls lived in the other direction, and Cassie offered to walk with her and stay the night at hers, but Katy wasn't in the mood for guests. Anyway, Cassie snored, and Katy would hear it through the wall.

It was only a short way to her house, and she'd done it plenty of times before on her own. Cassie had whispered in her ear about the news, someone or other killing a woman called Felicity and two men, but it wasn't like they'd be out and about now, waiting for her. Christ, that was just stupid thinking.

She tottered off up the road, smiling at the sound of her friends' laughter fading the farther away she walked from them. Her high heels rubbed at the back.

Bet I've got a blister.

The stupid things were half a size too small, but she'd loved them so much and had bought them anyway. They pinched her toes, too, and the pain was getting a bit much. It was no good, she'd have to take them off. Bending, she removed one then the other, the relief instant. She carried them all the way to her house, her feet even sorer by the time she arrived, grit and dirt digging into her soles and scraping between her swollen toes. The wind had helped her along, pushing her from behind, and she shivered at the coldness of it and how it crept inside her coat to smother her skin with its icy fingers.

Katy let herself in and dropped her shoes on the floor, the clatter loud, and tossed her coat over the newel post. It slid to one side, looking drunker than her.

"Must put the chain across," she slurred, finding it a difficult task, seeing as there seemed to be two of them.

She weaved into the kitchen, slapping at the light switch, her reflection in the window giving her a bit of a fright until she realised it was herself.

"It's not a bloody killer out there, you silly cow," she said, turning on the tap to drink a glass of water, which was supposed to stop hangovers or something like that. The internet was full of useful snippets.

Finished drinking, she flicked off the light and dragged her arse to bed, flopping down in her clothes. She was too piddled to get under the covers, but she'd forgotten to turn the heating off, so it was warm enough. With the world spinning, she closed her eyes and battled the urge to be sick.

She had a dream where she was tied to the bedposts, her body a star shape. She tugged at the bonds, and they grated on her skin. Rope? While she wasn't scared, she'd let the dream play out, but if it got weird, she'd force herself awake, something she'd done many a time. Looking about, she blinked at the sight of opaque plastic hanging from the ceiling, creating a tent around her bed. Her furniture beyond presented as murky shapes, but she easily made out the wardrobe, the chest of drawers, and…

Someone was standing in the bedroom doorway, the light from the landing shining behind them.

Katy waited to see whether it was her dream lover coming to do all sorts of sexy things to her, and if he wasn't her cup of tea, she'd just make things go in another direction. The person came closer and stood at the bottom of the bed, then parted two lengths of the plastic and stared inside through the gap.

It was a woman, blonde, with a hoodie and black jeans on. She held a knife, pointing it towards Katy, whose heart picked up speed, and she wondered whether she ought to cut the dream short now before it got nasty and frightened her. Her brain was still foggy, though, from all that alcohol, and when the woman climbed on the bed and straddled her, she wasn't sure what to think.

"What do you want?" she said, doing what she always did in these sorts of dreams where she was aware it wasn't real and could engage with the characters.

"I don't want anything except you dead," the woman said in a man's voice.

Weird AF.

Katy thought about giggling, but the woman's face was so fixed, so expressionless, it put the shits up her and scared the laughter away. The eyes didn't sit in the sockets right either, recessed and beady. The mouth had a slit between the lips, and the tip of a tongue pressed through it.

It was time to wake up now.

She pushed herself into consciousness, but nothing changed. Was this actually happening? Katy's stomach churned, and again she willed herself to wake but with the same result. She was still drunk, that was it, and on top of that, hallucinating.

The woman was heavy on her, and she leant over so her nose rested on Katy's. The scent of rubber and shampoo wafted, and she stared into the woman's eyes, trying to read any form of emotion.

They were as blank as her face.

"Get off me," Katy said, bucking and tugging at the bonds.

The woman gripped the knife in both hands and aimed it downwards. It seemed to move in slow motion, south towards her belly, then the blade disappeared inside it, and Katy stared, fascinated that it didn't hurt. Not until it was pulled out then pushed in again. She wet herself, the hot liquid coating her inner thighs, then going cold as it sank into the quilt. The woman raised the knife again, high, and brought it down.

"Three," she said, the word a rasp.

And she kept on counting, kept stabbing, and Katy felt more than drunk now. She floated on an ocean of pain, telling herself to pull out of the nightmare, and when that didn't happen, she whispered, "See it through. It'll be over soon, and I'll wake up."

"It will be over soon," the woman said. "This wouldn't have happened if you'd said yes." A pause. A stab. "Ten…"

"What?" She was fading, bobbing in that void between life and death. Was this what it felt like to die?

"At Vicky's Café, I offered to buy you a coffee, and you said no."

Katy would have frowned if her forehead listened to her, but it ignored her. "I don't… I don't understand…" No woman had asked to get her a drink.

"You should have just let me buy it. Just let me be your friend. That's all I wanted, a friend." She hissed. "Eleven."

Then came punches, each one bringing on an agony Katy had never experienced before. It wrung out her stomach in wickedly spiteful hands, and she groaned.

"That hurt, does it?" the woman asked.

Katy had no breath left in her to answer.

The rest of the stabs came quickly then, the attacker whispering the numbers until she reached twenty-three. Katy's stomach was so hot, with the pain of the slices and the heat of blood that seeped and pumped and oozed and spurted. It dripped down her sides onto the bedding, and she stupidly wondered how she'd get the stain out. Then her mind faded, her thoughts disappearing, leaving her head a blank space, full of blackness and a strange buzzing noise. Was that her life fizzing out? Her mind shorting?

She stared at the woman, who had an electric toothbrush in her hand instead of the knife, and she dipped it into Katy's belly then brought it to her mouth and brushed her teeth. Now Katy knew this wasn't real, that it was a nightmare, and if she just watched it play out, she'd jolt upright in bed, and none of the blood would be there, none of the stab wounds, the pain, and no weird woman.

She closed her eyes and waited for that moment to come.

He folded the plastic into squares this time so none of the blood could escape. He'd brought a black bag up with him earlier and set about putting all the messy shields into it. Some of the ceiling paint had come off when he'd torn at the duct tape holding the tent in place, but that was neither here nor there.

With the refuse bag out in the garden beside his plastic roll and backpack, he walked around her house and, with fresh gloves on, touched and caressed her belongings, imagining what it was like to live there. It wasn't really a place he'd think of as home, too sterile and modern, nothing like the comfort of Den's. Agitated that he couldn't get the same sense of contentment, he left the house and collected his things, then walked away, down the alley and onto the cliff top. He had one more person on his list, and getting rid of him was a burning urge inside him. The wanker didn't live full time in Smaltern and wasn't due back from his fancy job abroad until the day after tomorrow.

That was okay. He needed a break. All this activity had wrung him out, and he could do with a bit of time to process what he'd do once he'd killed them all. He'd move away, from the memories, the pain, go somewhere he could start again, where no one looked at him funny and thought he was weird.

Somewhere he could be loved.

Somewhere he was important.

CHAPTER SIXTEEN

The residue of her nightmare had lingered all through her dinner with Zach last night. She'd ended up explaining that she suffered with bad dreams, usually about Uthway and what he'd done to her. Zach had been kind and supportive, as she'd known he would be, and as she pounded her feet on the treadmill, Andy huffing and puffing on another beside her, she acknowledged she'd struck lucky in getting together with the ME.

She switched the machine off, her calf muscles burning, and moved on to the elliptical, for her sins. After ten minutes, she'd had enough, and went over to tap Andy on the shoulder.

"We'd better get going if we want to eat," she said.

Once they'd showered and had breakfast in the leisure centre café, she drove towards work, sighing at the case and how nothing seemed to be coming together. What did the number twenty-three mean? And the witch? She so wanted to believe there was just one killer, but with Jean Salter saying it had been a woman at Felicity's, Helena couldn't really discount that—unless the old woman was mistaken.

"Shall we pop to see Jean again later?" she asked.

"Jean?" Andy clearly wasn't with it yet.

"Salter. The old dear who saw the lady in the street."

"Ah. Why?" He sipped from his to-go cup of coffee.

"To question her again to see if she's sure of what she saw. She's old…"

"But she was 'with it' from what I remember. All right, she went off on a tangent, but otherwise she was okay."

"Hmm." He was right. "So what then?" She sighed again, at a loss.

"I don't know. Keep trawling through their pasts, questioning people who knew them? Maybe Ol will find something to do with witches. It wouldn't surprise me if the number is linked with it."

"Talking to everyone who knew them… Think about it. That's basically the whole of Smaltern regarding Den. That'll be a lot of man hours, and we don't have that many men. It'll take weeks, and in the meantime, he or she could kill again." She turned into the station car park, frustrated beyond belief.

Louise was standing by the back door, sucking on her vape.

"We're not that early, are we?" Helena switched the engine off. "She only usually smokes that before work and on her breaks."

"Nope, it's two minutes to eight. Maybe she's having a sneaky breather while it's quiet."

Louise started work at seven, so if breakfast for those in the holding cells was already done and dusted, Helena couldn't blame her for needing something to calm her nerves. Some detainees were nothing short of arseholes and would test even a saint's patience.

They got out of the car, Helena pressing the key button to blip the doors locked. She walked towards Louise, who smiled with what appeared to be relief.

"Thank God you're here, guv. I need someone to talk to."

"What's the matter? Are you all right?"

Louise was paler than usual, and her hand holding the vape shook. "It's been a horrible hour waiting for you to come in. There's been another one. A stabbing, I mean."

"Oh, for fuck's sake!" This was doing her head in. "How many is this bastard going to kill before we catch him?"

The outside light above the door showcased Louise's watery eyes. "It's one of us who's been stabbed." Her lips wobbled, and she raised the vape to take an almighty puff. She blew out cherry-scented smoke.

Helena's brain stalled for a moment. "What?" Her guts rolled over. "Who?"

"Clive."

"Oh my God…" Helena's skin went ice cold, and she struggled to breathe for a second or two, her chest tight.

"How?" Andy asked.

"That's the fucking thing," Louise said, voice full of venom. "He spotted that bloody killer last night and followed him—well, about two this morning. He called in the fact he was tailing someone carrying a roll of plastic, of all things, and he thought it best to check out where he was going. Clive was parked in his car down Gold Street after sorting a domestic, and the bloke walked out from the cliff between two houses and then turned a corner, disappearing into the Seaview estate. Clive caught up with him, and the bloke dumped his stuff over a wall then climbed over. Clive did the same, and the man was waiting for him on the other side. He stabbed him, grabbed his gear, and ran."

"Why the hell wasn't I called?" Helena asked.

"Because Clive isn't dead, and the killer fucked off somewhere."

"Is Clive going to be all right?" Helena couldn't get over this. It was all so bloody disturbing.

"He had an op overnight, and I rang the hospital in an official capacity just now. They said he'll be fine. It didn't affect any major organs, it just went into his stomach, and not all the way either. About three inches."

"Three inches too many," Helena snapped. "Sorry, I don't mean to take it out on you. Christ, this is just…"

"I know, but get this…" Louise scratched her head. "While Clive was on the grass after being stabbed, he called it in. He gave a description."

Talk about swings and roundabouts. While Helena was shocked and upset that Clive had been attacked, she was elated he'd clocked what his assailant looked like. And him having that roll of plastic, it was bound to be their killer, wasn't it? Or at least Mark and Den's. Was he using that to stop the blood spatter from spreading? It made sense.

Or maybe I'm clutching at straws.

"What time was he stabbed?" Andy asked.

"Around two."

They all went inside, and Helena ordered Louise to have a sweet cup of tea. In the incident room, she sat at a spare desk and tapped her fingers on it while Andy accessed the information logged about Clive being stabbed.

"From this description, the bloke matches who we saw on CCTV," Andy said.

"Good. The height?"

"Yep, same as what Tom told you."

"Okay. So what we need to determine now is whether he was going to a victim's house or leaving it and was on his way home."

Ol and Phil came in, and Helena passed on the news.

"Fucking hell," Phil muttered. "It's getting personal now, picking one of our own." He slumped into his chair, a puff of breath coming out of him.

"Do your thing with the map," Helena said to him, waving at his computer. "He was spotted in Darby Road to begin with, then he turned to go farther into the estate and jumped over a wall. I want all the streets within a two-mile radius."

"Okay, guv." Phil got to work.

Ol was still standing by the doorway. She'd gone white. "Darby Road is near where my friend lives."

"Is it? If you're worried about her, give her a ring." Helena smiled sympathetically. The killer could be targeting anyone, whatever age or sex, so she could understand Ol being concerned.

"I will. Bear with me, I have a hangover, even though I only drank two glasses of wine." Ol walked over to her desk and pulled her mobile out of her handbag. She pushed her hair out of her eyes.

"Good night, was it?" Helena asked, grinning despite the severity of the situation.

"My friend's hen do." She swiped her screen and lifted the phone to her ear, tapping her fingertips on her knee. "We had a bloody good laugh. I should go out more often, but I'm always too knackered." She frowned. "There's no answer. She had a fair few drinks, so I expect she's slept through her alarm or is driving."

"I'll pretend I didn't hear that," Helena said in jest. "She might still be under the influence. Try her home phone?"

"I don't have it. I'll look it up. She's not due at work until nine, so I'll ring her there as well."

"Why are you so worried? I know there's a killer out there, but it's highly doubtful he'd have gone for her. You were all together, weren't you?"

Ol winced. "That's the thing. She walked home by herself."

"Oh fuck…"

"I told our other friend, Cassie, to tell her about the murders, but Katy still went off by herself."

"Where were you?"

"The Villager's Inn." Ol bit her lip.

"Right, so that's close by Darby Road. Look, if it'll make you feel better, me and Andy will go round there now, okay? Not the usual thing to do, but I can't stand the thought of you fretting all day. What's her address?"

Ol logged on and accessed the information. "Fifteen Scribbins Avenue."

"Come on." Helena got up and poked Andy in the arm.

"Thanks," Ol said. "I'm probably just being silly, but Cassie said Katy had been bothered recently by some bloke."

"In what way?"

"Oh, she saw him a lot in various places."

Helena thought of Marshall and how he'd done the same to her. She shivered. "Anything else?"

"He went into Vicky's Café and asked to buy her a coffee. She said he was odd, like he stooped over her, and his eyes were strange. Recessed. Beady. She told him no thanks, and he said she'd regret saying no to him. I told her last night to report it if she saw him again and it was obvious he'd followed her."

"That's about all the advice you could have given, so don't worry about it." Helena walked to the doorway. "We'll be back in a few, all right? Keep trying her on the phone."

She left the station with Andy in tow, the car still faintly warm from where they'd been in it before. Just as she buckled up, the wind pushed at the vehicle, and the rain came down.

"Bloody weather," she said and set off for Scribbins Avenue.

"Do you think this is warranted?" Andy asked.

"Do I eff. I'm just doing it for Ol. You know how she gets when something bothers her. She'll be off her game all day and, for purely selfish reasons, I don't want her to be. We need her on top form."

"Makes sense."

"Besides, it's only a quick trip. We'll see she's all right then get back to work. By the time we do, Phil will have found out all the streets we need to focus on. Our killer lives in one of them, probably on the other side of that wall."

She still couldn't believe the fucker had stabbed Clive. Then again, the fear of getting caught would have spurred him on. He was lucky Clive was going to pull through, otherwise he'd have a harsher time of it once he was nicked than he usually would. Coppers looked after each other.

Outside number fifteen, she cut the engine and reached into the back seat, collecting them both a pair of gloves. "Just in case."

They walked up Katy's path. The front door was ajar, which was alarming, so she raised her eyebrows at Andy: *We're going in?*

He nodded, stepping inside first.

Helena followed. A pair of high heels had been left beside the door, and a coat hung skew-whiff on the newel post. She used her elbow to push the door to.

Helena called out, "Katy?"

With no answer, they stuck together and checked the downstairs rooms. The back door in the kitchen had been jimmied, and slithers of wood were scattered on the mat. She glanced at Andy, and he grimaced.

"Shit," he whispered.

"Why break in through the back then presumably leave through the front?" she whispered in return. "Unless Katy heard him coming in and escaped out the front way? In that case, why didn't she call it in?"

Andy shrugged and pointed to the ceiling. She nodded and tailed him up the stairs. All the doors were closed. Andy slid his gloves on, as did Helena, then he opened the doors until only one was left. Helena took a deep breath. She had an uneasy feeling in the pit of her stomach. While it might not have been a killer who'd broken in, that front door being open wasn't right.

Andy turned the handle and pushed the door wide.

A wicked stench billowed out.

"Oh my fucking God!" Helena closed her eyes for a moment, a finger beneath her nostrils, and when she opened them again, the scene was unfortunately still there.

It was reminiscent of Felicity's. The woman on the bed had been tied to it, and her stomach was a wreck. Her top had been pulled up to below her breasts, exposing the slashes and stabs. Her insides poked through. Her face hadn't been touched as far as Helena could tell, although blood flecked it, giving the impression she was covered in burnt-red moles.

Helena glanced away while Andy continued to stare, his breaths coming out heavy. She studied the walls, looking for that fucking witch drawing and the number, but so far, all she'd picked up was blood. It formed a rectangle behind the bed, perfect lines either side where something had been put up. She glanced at the ceiling at the spatter there and a patch where paint had been ripped off.

Her tummy hurt. She was that sick of this — of all of it. What kind of maniac were they dealing with? And what the hell was the reason for this?

Was it the man who'd been following Katy? Had he followed all the others, too?

She took her phone out and rang Ol. "Hi."

"Is she all right?" Her voice wavered.

Helena took a deep breath. "I'm afraid not, love."

"What?" It wasn't a shriek but a quiet query.

"Sorry, Ol, but he's got to her."

"Oh my God!" Ol's breathing was erratic. "Stabbed?"

"Yes."

"That fucking bastard!" A small sob filtered through the connection.

"Do you need to go home?" Helena asked.

"Fuck no. I'm going to help bloody find him. I'm not close enough to her for it to be a conflict of interest. I just feel sorry for Cassie. They've been best friends for years."

"Okay, what day and date did the man offer to buy Katy a coffee in the café? Can you remember?"

"Last month sometime. I don't know when. Oh God... I can't think!" A pause, more erratic breathing. "Hang on... It was a weekday, because she'd gone to Vicky's for her lunch. She said she had lasagne and it was on special, so that's a Wednesday. I go there sometimes for that."

"Fantastic. If you're sure you're up to it, request CCTV footage if they have any for inside the shop, and there will definitely be some for outside. Check every Wednesday, going back two months, okay? Two. Does she have family around here?"

"I don't know. She's mainly Cassie's friend. I only see her when we get together. We're mates, but not like that. I'll run a check."

"Right, and if you find anyone, text me the name and address. We're going to be a while."

"Shit, shit, shit."

"I know. I'm so sorry."

"Me, too. I need to get on. We have to find him."

Helena ended the call then rang Phil. "Don't let Ol know it's me. Keep an eye on her, will you? We're here, and it isn't good."

"Okay, Benny. A drink sounds great," Phil said.

"Good thinking, making out I'm your brother. Watch her for me. I just rang her, so she knows Katy's dead. In case she suddenly has a meltdown, I've asked her to get CCTV from Vicky's Café for the past two months. We're looking at Wednesday lunchtimes. That was when the bloke asked to buy her a coffee."

"What time shall I meet you then, Benny?"

"You're good at this."

"Cheers. Catch you later."

"Tarra." She sighed and rang Louise. "Hi. We're at fifteen Scribbins Avenue. Residence of a

Katy someone—I don't know her last name. She's been stabbed, same as the others, so can you ring around and get balls rolling? Me and Andy will stay here until SOCO and Zach arrive."

It came to something when she saw her boyfriend more at work than outside of it.

"Blimey," Louise said. "So that was most likely the killer who knifed Clive then."

"It's looking that way, but we have a break of sorts. Someone has been following Katy, and we have some dates we can poke into, thank God, and maybe find him on CCTV. We're getting closer. I've got to go."

"All right, guv. I'll sort everything now."

CHAPTER SEVENTEEN

Helena slid her phone in her pocket. She didn't want to step into the bedroom as she didn't have booties on, so while Andy stayed at the bedroom doorway, she went to the car and got some. The rain had stopped, but the ground was still wet, so she'd have to put the booties on inside. In the hallway, she placed them over her shoes, put Andy's in her pocket, and glanced back outside. A man came out of next door, and she smiled when he turned her way, giving her the once-over, his gaze stopping on her feet.

He frowned.

"Hi. I'm DI Helena Stratton." She showed him her ID. "Do you know the resident of this address?" She jerked her thumb at Katy's door.

He was around fifty, with thinning grey hair and a white goatee. He stroked it while thinking.

What's there to bloody think about? You either know her or you don't!

"Not really. I've only been here for two weeks—I live alone. I've seen her coming and going, and she's said hello once or twice." He stared at her feet again. "Um…" He pointed at them.

"Did you hear anything last night?" she asked, hoping he'd be able to give her something.

"Only her going out. I looked through the window as I was closing the blinds and saw her walking down the street all dolled up. I assumed she was going out for a drink or something."

"Did you hear her come home?"

"No, I went to bed about nine-thirty. Had an awful headache. Is everything all right?" He frowned harder, appearing genuinely worried.

"Nothing for you to concern yourself with, sir." She smiled, and to call an end to the conversation, she added, "Thanks for your time."

He waved awkwardly and strode down his path. A police car arrived, and the neighbour glanced back at her over his shoulder, eyebrows raised, then got into his Ford and drove off. She'd bet he'd be thinking about their encounter all day.

Two uniforms came up to her, and she briefed them. "It appears to be the same bloke, but if anyone mentions seeing a blonde lady, don't discount it. So, door-to-door, please. Ah, here's SOCO." She briefed them, too, then followed them up the stairs, passing the booties to Andy on the landing. "I've just spoken to the neighbour on the right. Nothing except he saw her go out. She was alone and walked. 'Dolled up' as he put it."

"Why aren't I surprised he didn't know much?"

She shrugged. "We ought to be used to dead ends by now. Anyway, two uniforms are here, so I've sent them on door-to-door. Maybe something will come up there. You never know, a miracle might happen."

Andy shook his head. "We'll be strapped for officers at this rate, because you can bet your life there'll be a few out this morning where Clive got stabbed, doing the same thing, probably getting no bleedin' answers."

She sighed — a constant in her life lately — and watched a SOCO take photographs. "See anything in amongst that blood on the walls?"

The SOCO glanced at her. "Like the pictures from the other places?"

"Yes."

"Hang on."

He walked closer to the bed and peered at the red patterns. It seemed to go on forever, him looking, but at last he pointed. "Just there."

"Can I come in?" she asked.

"Let me just take some pictures of the doorway and carpet there, then you can."

Helena and Andy stepped to either side to get out of shot.

"Come on then," the SOCO said and beckoned her in.

She walked to the head of the bed, forcing her attention to the wall and not Katy. Leaning over, she stared, the stench of dried blood and dried urine rising to greet her. She bit back a gag. There, the same size as the others, was a pencil drawing of a witch's face, the number twenty-three above it.

"What the hell are you telling us?" she whispered and drew back to text Ol. She needed to remind her to also look into witches this morning. It might have slipped her mind, seeing as this had happened.

Her reply came back quickly: *Okay. Her mum lives at nineteen Bassett Road. Valerie Watkins. Her dad, Stuart, lives in Sheffield.*

Helena typed back: *Are you up for seeing a picture of her? We need to make sure it's her.*

Ol: *Yes.*

Helena snapped one of Katy's face then sent it along. Ol came back with a simple 'yes', and

Helena messaged her to hold off contacting Sheffield police to tell Katy's father until they'd had a chance to visit the mother.

Zach appeared, and she smiled at him.

"This is just too much for words," he said and approached the body. He took a packaged thermometer out of his bag.

While he did the business, Helena did her usual and glanced around the room. She thought about Katy still wearing her clothes. The poor woman hadn't even had a chance to get her pyjamas on. Had the killer dragged her up here and forced her to get on the bed? She wasn't under the covers, so that was highly likely.

Christ. The idea of Katy being terrified out of her wits was something Helena didn't want to think about, but she did anyway. How could she not when presented with such a gruesome scene?

"I'm estimating around midnight," Zach said.

"Okay, you might not have heard, but Clive got stabbed about two a.m. He was following who we think is our killer."

"Jesus." Zach shone a slim torch onto Katy's stomach.

"So the timeline fits. He was here, then he was going home. Two secs." She rang Phil. "Concentrate on the direction the man was going, not where he was coming from. Get

CCTV of the area. I'm betting he was on his way home."

"On it, guv."

Phone in her pocket again, she moved away from the bed. The smell was getting to her. "We're going to have to leave you to it," she said to Zach. "We've got a mother to visit."

Helena and Andy left the house and, taking a moment in the car, she phoned Louise. "Have you any news on the uniforms asking questions on the estate where Clive was attacked?"

"Nothing yet."

"Bugger. Thanks." Next, she rang Phil again. "It's me. I forgot to ask... Is Ol holding up okay?"

"All right."

"Good. I know you usually ring when you've found something, but..."

"Nothing yet. Just waiting for a movie to arrive from Amazon."

Good. He was playing the game again, pretending.

"The CCTV?" she asked.

"Yeah. Taking a while."

"We're off to Katy's mum's place, so don't expect us back for another hour or so. Find out where Katy worked and sort out someone to go and question the employees. Shit, we could do with another person. Good job we have Evan joining us soon."

"Yeah, I heard it was a good plot. I like a bit of action, me."

"I'll let you get on."

She drove away, heading for Bassett Road. "Slow as anything."

"What is?" Andy asked.

"Getting information. We're so bloody close yet miles away, know what I mean?"

"Yep. Still, we'll get him."

"Providing the cameras even work outside Vicky's Café. If they don't, I'll know damn well the universe is against us."

"They can't all be broken."

"No, but this is a small town, so funds for that sort of thing get pushed to the wayside. Let's just hope we have a bit of luck now. If we can spot Katy going into the café, we can look for who else went in there as well. Shit. Ring Louise for me, will you? I need officers to go to The Villager's Inn and ask for names of people who were there last night. I'm not saying the manager will know everyone, but he's got to know some, surely."

Andy made the call, and Helena parked outside Valerie Watkins' house. She took a moment to gather her wits. There had been too much death the last few days, what with the Walker sisters and the new murders. It was bound to filter through to the main news stations soon, then no one would want to bloody visit for a holiday come the summer. She shouldn't be thinking of it in those terms, but Yarworth was bound to, the higher-ups breathing down his neck, then he'd have to breathe down hers, and she shuddered at the thought.

"Louise is doing it now," Andy said, shoving his phone in his jacket pocket.

Helena stared at her hands, at his, then into the footwells. "Blimey, we still have our booties and gloves on."

They removed them, and Helena popped them on the back seat. She could procrastinate by bothering everyone on the phone, asking for updates, but it wouldn't stop her having to make the next step. She'd have to speak to Valerie Watkins no matter what, so she took a deep breath and left the car.

With Andy by her side, she walked up the path and knocked on the door. A young blond lad answered, about nineteen or so, and cocked his head.

"Yeah?" he said, his white T-shirt marked with lines where it had been ironed then folded.

"Is Valerie Watkins in?"

He raised his eyebrows and looked Helena up and down. Assessing what sort of person she was and why she was there?

Probably.

"I'll just get her." He turned and walked up the hallway. "Mum! Door!"

A woman came down the stairs, and there wasn't any resemblance to Katy at all. Maybe her daughter took after her dad. Her black hair sat high in a ponytail, and it seemed they'd disturbed her doing her makeup. Only one eye had black liner on the top lid. She could pass for thirty if not for the lines beside her eyes and mouth.

Helena produced her ID and introduced them. "May we come in? It's about Katy."

Valerie went white and sucked in a sharp breath. "Is she all right?"

Helena smiled tightly and gestured to be let in. She stepped inside, and Andy came in behind her, closing the door. Again, Helena gestured, indicating they go through into the living room on the right.

"Sit down, Mrs Watkins."

She did, on a coffee-coloured corduroy sofa with sagging cushions at the back. Andy remained standing by the door while Helena sat in a chair at an angle to the sofa so she could clearly see Valerie's face.

"What's happened?" Valerie asked, gaze darting from Helena to Andy then back again.

"We're investigating a person who seems to have been following Katy around. Has she told

215

you about this?" Helena laced her fingers in her lap.

"No, she hasn't mentioned it." Valerie wrung her hands.

The lad came in and plonked himself in the other chair. "Not earwigging or anything, but she told me. Some bellend asked her if he could buy her a coffee or something. She said he'd been turning up wherever she was, and he went up to her in the café. She told him no, and he got arsey with her, said he just wanted to be mates."

"When was this?" Helena asked, praying for an actual date to save Phil having to trawl through umpteen Wednesdays of CCTV.

"About a month ago."

Relieved the timeline matched what Ol had said, Helena relaxed a little. "Did she tell you what he looked like?"

"Nah, just that he was a weirdo."

"Why wouldn't she tell me?" Valerie asked, staring around at everyone.

"Because you worry too much, Mum. Katy reckoned he was just some dickhead, end of. I told her if he bothered her again to ring me and I'd go and sort him out."

Valerie glared at him as if telling him with her eyes he ought to watch his language in front of the police. "But if he was following her, he's more than just a…what you said."

"Is there anyone you can think of who this might be?" It was a long shot, but Helena had to try. "An old school friend? A work colleague?"

The lad shrugged. "Like I said, just some weirdo."

"Mrs Watkins?" Helena prodded, sensing it was hopeless to even ask.

Valerie shook her head. "I have no idea. Since she moved out, we don't see her much, maybe once a fortnight, if that. She doesn't tell me anything except what she gets up to with her friends, and even then that's only with me asking what she's been doing. I don't think she'd share if I didn't ask."

Crap. I should have got Ol to contact her friends. "We know Katy's best friend is someone called Cassie. Do you know where she lives?"

"She lives in Dean Street," the lad said. "Can't remember the number, but it's the only one with a red door, halfway down the road. I had to drop Katy off there once when she'd been here for Sunday dinner. They were going to The Villager's after."

"Thank you," Helena said. "This next question is distressing, and I'm sorry to have to ask it, but do you know of anyone who'd want to harm Katy? Has she had an argument with someone recently; has she mentioned a grudge?"

"You what?" the lad said, scowling. "Are you saying someone's hurt my bloody sister?"

"Charlie…" Valerie warned.

"Because if they have, I don't get why. Katy's great," Charlie said. "Everyone likes her."

Just as I was expecting. Helena held back a sigh. She may as well break the news now. "I'm sorry to inform you, but we have reason to believe Katy was murdered last night."

Charlie shot out of his seat and sat beside his mum. He shook all over, while Valerie screamed. He hugged her, crying, and Helena had to turn away. She looked at Andy, who lowered his head—yes, this was the rotten part of their job. He walked off to make the usual sweet tea. Helena never spoke while he was doing it. There was no point. Valerie and Charlie continued crying, gripping each other as grief swept over them, and Helena felt like she was intruding just by being there.

Andy returned and put the cups on a side table, and it seemed to pull Valerie from wherever she'd gone inside her mind. She untangled herself from her son and reached for a cup, handing it to him.

"Drink that, love," she said. "The sugar will help."

Helena guessed the woman was putting her own upset aside in order to be strong for her son, and she admired her greatly for it. A lump rose in her throat, and she had to blink to stop any tears forming.

Valerie straightened her spine and sniffed. "Is it the same person doing it as the one mentioned on the news?" She sounded no-nonsense, all business.

"We believe so, yes." Helena gave a wan smile.

"What is going on around here?" Valerie hugged Charlie with one arm while he sipped tea and stared at the carpet. "So many people killed in a matter of days. This used to be a safe place, for God's sake." Then, "Would she have suffered for long?"

Helena wasn't going to lie. "I don't know if it was quick. The medical examiner is with her now."

"Where did it happen?" Charlie croaked, his face red and blotchy.

"At her home."

"Did she take someone back with her?" he asked. "She was on a hen do last night. I was at the same bloody pub with my mates. She was fine. No one was bothering her."

Helena perked up. "Were you there the whole time?"

"No, I got there at seven and left just after nine."

"Did you see anyone acting suspiciously?" *Please have noticed something.* "Someone watching her?"

Charlie shook his head. "It was full of regulars, the hen party, and me and my mates. There wasn't anyone there who would have done...done that to her."

"Can you recall everyone who was there?"

"I'll try."

Charlie reeled off names, and Andy wrote them down, then left the room. Helena guessed he was calling the names in to Ol and Phil.

"Do you know how she got home?" Valerie asked quietly.

"She walked alone. We believe she got there safe. Unfortunately, it appears someone broke in via the back door."

Valerie wailed at that. "My poor baby. She would have been so scared."

Helena excused herself to phone Dave Lund, their distress too raw to witness. He said he'd be with them inside ten minutes. She returned to the living room and explained an officer would be there shortly to help them through this difficult time. Valerie drank her tea, staring into space, and Charlie did likewise.

Once Dave turned up and introductions were made, she left the FLO to it. He was excellent at his job and would ease Valerie and Charlie into the next steps with calm and grace. They couldn't be in better hands.

CHAPTER EIGHTEEN

He woke up panicked, recalling what had happened last night. He wouldn't have stabbed that copper if he hadn't chased him. They'd be on to him soon, and he hadn't finished what he'd set out to do. There was one more left. Would he be able to kill him before he got that knock on the door?

"Fucking hell," he muttered, getting out of bed and padding downstairs, scratching his crotch then stopping because it reminded him of Eddie.

He made cereal for breakfast on autopilot, his mind on that knife going into the copper's belly. He'd jabbed it in just enough to shock the bloke so he could run away. He'd gone straight home—if he'd walked the streets for a bit, he'd have been picked up in no time. Better that he hide out at home than get stopped by another patrol and have to explain why he was carrying a sodding roll of plastic sheeting and had blood on him.

At the kitchen table, he ate, sifting through his feelings. While he didn't have any remorse for stabbing the pig, he did have anger simmering. The incident could mean everything would be cut short if they stepped up the search for him — which they would, considering he'd had the audacity to attack one of their own.

He imagined moving away now, today, to start that new life he'd promised himself, but allowing the other bloke on his list to live meant he'd torment himself with his freedom for the rest of his days. He'd always be there in the back of his mind, whispering, "No…no…no."

He couldn't deal with that.

Soon it would all be over, and he could walk away with no regrets.

Mum was wailing about Eddie going missing. She slung more alcohol down her throat and kicked at a magazine half hanging off the table. It fell to the floor he'd hoovered a few hours ago, and anger boiled inside him.

Eddie had been gone for six months now, so why couldn't she just get over it? Her drink intake had got worse, and she'd lost her bloody job and all. He was sick of paying the bills, sick of having nothing left of his wages except for enough to have a pint in The Villager's every night.

She was a selfish bitch, only thinking of herself like that.

He stared at her, and a red mist descended, forcing him to yank her by the arm and haul her standing. She swayed, pissed as she was, and stared at him, her eyes glassy.

"We're going out," he said.

She spluttered. "But it's the middle of the night."

"Yeah, when normal people are in bed. You woke me up with your fucking crying, you loud cow. You need a walk."

He'd already got dressed, having had enough of listening to her, the plan sinking into his head fully formed. The nighttime express was due at three-forty, and it didn't stop at Smaltern station, just breezed through on the way to Scotland. She still had her clothes on from the daytime, slippers instead of shoes, but that would just add to the authenticity. She'd wandered out, alone, drunk, and flung herself onto the tracks, that was what they'd say.

He grabbed the mask and blonde wig from a kitchen cupboard. Eddie had bought them once the police had gathered he'd worn the witch one to rob Den's, saying it was a good idea to keep wearing them. He put them on and returned to the living room.

Mum stared at him and whimpered. "Why are you wearing…?"

"Shut your face. I've had as much of you as I can take."

He guided her outside, closing the front door quietly so the neighbours didn't hear it, and kept to the shadows as he tugged her along the street. The station was only five minutes away, but it took fifteen, what with her staggering. He didn't take her to the actual station but through a field, the track hidden behind a long row of bushes. He shoved her through and followed her out to the other side.

"What are we doing here?" she asked, the words elongated and floaty in the darkness. The moonlight shone on her, and she teetered, holding her hands out for balance.

"You'll see."

He cracked his fist against her temple, and she went down, hitting her skull on the rocky verge. She was out cold, and if she hadn't been, he'd have kept punching her until she was. He carried her to the track and placed her down, then went back to the hedge to hide behind it and watch.

The rumble of the express was music to his ears, and he stared into the gloom, waiting for the headlamps to pierce the night and illuminate the woman who'd given birth to him but hadn't cared about him at all.

The train went by too fast for him to see what it did to her, but once it had continued into the distance, slowing to a stop, he couldn't hang around to inspect his handiwork. He walked home, lighter of heart than he'd been in years, and thought about how Eddie and Mum had treated him. Then his mind went to all the others who'd pissed him off, rejecting him, giving him the sense he wasn't important to anyone, anywhere.

And his plan was born.

CHAPTER NINETEEN

In the incident room, everyone crowded around Phil's computer. CCTV had come up trumps, and they were looking at the image of Katy Watkins just about to enter Vicky's Café on a Wednesday last month at one-thirty. The footage had been paused, showing her with one hand on the door and one leg bent, ready to step inside.

"Play it slowly," Helena said.

Phil clicked it to resume, and Katy walked into the café. The camera was pointing directly at the building, and Phil had enlarged it so they could see what was going on better. Two minutes of waiting passed, Katy presumably at the till placing her order, then appeared again. The café had a high table running the length of the window, and she sat on a stool and tucked in, eating some lasagne. She had a cup in front of her, and a woman browsed on her phone beside her, nibbling on a sandwich.

A man walked along the street and stopped outside the café, staring in. The hairs on Helena's neck rose. His body was similar to the man in the alley out the back of Den's, but his hair was longer. Unfortunately, she couldn't see his face as his back was to the camera.

Phil paused it. "Look…" He pointed at the window. "His reflection."

"Fucking hell," Helena said. "Take a shot of the frame and blow it up in a minute. I want to see what happens next first. It might not even be him." But her gut said it was.

Phil pressed Play.

The man went inside and straight to Katy, to the side where no one else sat, and leant over her, caging her in. She glanced up at him, easing her head back to get some space between them, and his lips moved, maybe him asking if he could buy her a coffee. Katy's expression changed from confusion to annoyance, then he spoke again. Her face switched to fear, and he reared back, stared at her, then stalked away.

He didn't leave the café, but Katy did, scurrying up the street, clutching her bag strap as though she thought the man would come out and rob her. He followed then, at a distance, and she glanced over her shoulder, spotting him. Then she went out of shot.

"Bastard," Helena snapped. "Get that reflection frame enlarged, please."

Phil did so, and while the image was grainy, the man's face was clear enough.

"Fuck me sideways," Phil said, peering closer. "My brother went to school with that little twat."

"You what?" Helena's heart went crazy, banging hard and too fast, skipping a couple of beats. "Tell me you have a name."

Phil scrunched his eyes up in thought. "Can't bloody remember. Hang on, I'll ring my brother." He whipped his mobile out and placed the call. "Benny, who was that weird kid you went to school with, the one who always stank and stared at people? The skinny one who kept wanting to be your mate and didn't like it when you said no?" A pause. Phil scribbled down the name on his pad. "You're coming back a day early? Brilliant. It'll be good to see you. Does working in France suit you? Good. Anyway, speak soon. I have to go."

"Got you, Ian fucking Landon," Helena said, her legs going weak from the adrenaline rush. "Get his address, Ol." And to Phil, "Send that image to be enhanced. I want a clearer one if possible. Tell them it's urgent. Print off the one we've got for now."

"Ninety-four Sweetbriar Road," Ol called.

"Nothing bloody sweet about the man living there," Andy said.

Helena walked over to the printer and snatched the image out of the tray. "We need to speak to Louise to see if there are any uniforms handy. We're going to need backup for this. Come on, Andy."

She raced downstairs and slapped the image on the front desk, startling Louise.

"Him," Helena said. "He's likely the one we're after. Do a quick search for any priors for me, will you? Ian Landon, ninety-four Sweetbriar Road."

Louise tapped on her keyboard. "Nothing on him as far as crime goes. Doesn't mean he hasn't committed any, though, does it. Some of them are crafty bastards. Hang on a sec. I'll just check other people at that address." She typed in a command. "Three people, but what looks like his father left years ago. There's his mother, I assume, a Regina Landon, but she's deceased. And an Eddie Goddard who was reported as a missing person by Regina a long while back." She clicked her mouse. "The father's last known address is in Wigan, and he's also dead. Overdose."

So they had a loner to deal with. Great. They tended to be the worst. Too much time by themselves to plan things.

"Right, what about this Ian's workplace?" Helena was getting frustrated. She wanted immediate information. It wasn't coming at her fast enough.

Louise typed. "He's unemployed."

"So he has plenty of time to catch up on sleep when he's been out killing people at night, the wanker. What about other family members?"

Louise typed again. "Nothing, sorry."

Helena grabbed the image off the desk and scooted into the uniforms' break room. Five of them sat at the same table, drinking tea and having a good old gas.

"Guys, your break is over. I need you — now." She gave them the address and told them to park the police cars down the road out of sight. Holding up the image, she pointed to Landon's face. "We're after him for the recent murders and the attack on Clive, got it?"

They all stood at once, galvanised by her last few words.

"I'm going to be knocking on his door with Andy, but I want two of you round the back first, the other three with us at the front. I need to go and get a Taser, just in case, and you five won't have to do anything unless he gets lairy, all right? As far as he's concerned, I just want to ask him his whereabouts on the nights in question."

They nodded.

"See you there." She left the break room and grabbed Andy's elbow in reception. "I'm just going to sign a Taser out, then we'll be off. Casual call to begin with, just to gauge what to do next."

Taser in her possession, she led the way to the car, following the two police vehicles with the five uniforms inside. They did as she'd instructed and pulled up down the road, then got out. She parked directly outside Landon's house and walked along the street a bit.

She pointed at the biggest two men. "You two go round the back. There's an alleyway there, look."

The officers went that way and, once they were out of sight, she returned her attention to the others.

"You remain behind the bushes outside his house. I don't want him spooked seeing all of us. Me and Andy will be enough of a shock if he's the jumpy sort. Stay hidden until I either shout or you see things are getting out of hand. If we manage to get inside, I'll leave the door ajar. All clear?"

"Yes, guv."

She took a deep breath and strode to the front door, her trusty partner right beside her. Andy knocked, keeping it light, nothing to scare Landon into thinking they were there with arresting him in mind.

The door opened slightly, and the face of the man in the café window reflection appeared in the small gap. His eyes were set back and creepy, like they didn't belong in his head.

Helena smiled as though nothing was amiss and showed him her ID. She waited for him to bolt, but he just stared, opening the door a little wider.

"Hi. So sorry to bother you." *I'm bloody well not.* "I'm DI Helena Stratton, and this is DS Andy Mald. We're making enquiries in the area and were hoping you could help us. We have reason to believe someone we're looking for lives around this way, but to be honest, we have no clue where they actually live."

The man visibly relaxed. "What do you want from me then?"

"Can we come in? We're questioning the residents of every household in town, and it would be much easier to do inside so Andy here can take notes. Is that all right? It might rain again soon, and we wouldn't want his pad to get wet, would we. If you can't spare the time today, we can return tomorrow, or you can come down to the station at your convenience."

He blinked, seeming to think about that.

"To be fair," she went on, "it'll only take a few minutes, then we can get out of your hair. Like I said, we're talking to absolutely everyone who lives in Smaltern, so I'm afraid you'll just have to grin and bear it."

He stepped back and fully opened the door.

Helena and Andy went inside.

Helena shooed Landon with her hand. "In there will do." She wanted him out of the way so the door could be left open.

He walked into the living room, and Helena glanced at Andy then checked her Taser was hidden beneath her jacket. They followed him in, and he stood by the window, looking out.

"Want to take a seat?" she asked him.

"No." He lifted a shaking hand and threaded it through his hair.

"Okay. This won't take a minute." She blocked the doorway. "These are just standard questions, nothing to fret about." She stated the date and time of Felicity's murder. "Where were you on that night?"

He jolted but didn't stop staring outside. "Here. Asleep."

"Can anyone verify that?"

"No." He rolled his shoulders.

She gave the date and times of Mark's and Den's murders. "And that evening. Where were you?"

"Here."

"With anyone?"

"No."

What a surprise. "And what about last night? What were you doing then?"

"Here." He sniffed.

"And I assume no one can give you an alibi there either."

"No."

"Okay, not to worry. It's not like we think it's you, is it?" She watched for his reaction.

Nothing.

"I mean, I can be a hard woman in my job, but I'm not a total *witch.*"

A slight flinch, and he narrowed his eyes to slits. She hoped to God he couldn't see through that bloody hedge. It would fuck everything up if the uniforms were visible through the greenery.

"People say I'm like the one from *Snow White,*" she pushed, willing him to get angry or say something he shouldn't—something that would get him right in the shit. "You know, they reckon a wart on my nose would suit me. My team joke about it all the time. Actually, not all the time. Just *twenty-three* times. I'm drawing the line at wearing a pointy hat, though. I prefer witches without them, don't you?"

He didn't answer.

You cool bastard.

Time to switch it the other way. "Do you know any of the following people: Felicity

Greaves, Mark Simons, Den Simons, and Katy Watkins?"

He turned to look at her and grinned, and it was evil. Helena's skin crawled.

"Mark was a friend when we were kids, and I used to go round there for my tea. I know Den because he's his dad. I haven't heard the other two names."

Well, someone had suddenly swallowed a chatty pill, hadn't they.

"Did you hear about your friend's murder on the news?"

He maintained eye contact, but it was a bit too obvious. Like he wanted to prove he could do it. "Yeah. I haven't been mates with Mark in years, though, since we left secondary school, and I only see Den occasionally when I go to his shop. I used to like going up into their flat. It was like a proper home."

"I'm terribly sorry about their deaths. You must be upset?"

He gave the window his attention again, his smile gone, face shuttered. "No."

"Oh, did you have a falling out? Is that why you're not friends anymore?"

"No."

His monotone answers were getting on her tits. He seemed emotionless now, a switch flicking inside him to turn everything off.

"So you don't recognise the names of the women I mentioned?"

"No." He blinked, shoving his hands into his jean pockets.

She glanced at Andy to be on guard in case Landon brought out a weapon.

"I think you do know Katy," she went on, intending to reveal her hand. "You spoke to her in Vicky's Café last month." She told him the date and time. "She left soon after, and you followed her."

He shook his head imperceptibly and swallowed. "No."

"We have you on CCTV," she said. "What did you say to her to make her leave so quickly?"

He clamped his lips closed.

"It's just that when someone is murdered, even innocent meetings like the one in the café are called into question, and we have to follow it up." Why hadn't he asked her why she'd lied on the doorstep, saying they didn't know where the person they were looking for lived? "So I must have an answer, otherwise you'll have to come with us and answer them at the station. However faint your connection to Katy Watkins, you must explain yourself."

"I asked her if she wanted a coffee. She said no. End of story. No fairy tale for me."

What did he mean by that?

"Okay. Shall I make you some tea? It's always better to chat over a cuppa, isn't it? We'll get this cleared up in no time."

She looked at Andy, jerking her head for him to take her place at the door. Then she left the room and walked down the hallway into the kitchen. She clicked the kettle on—it already showed water through the transparent panel— and studied the right-hand side of the room. It was pristine—tidy and extremely clean, not a thing out of place.

Except for a blonde wig draped over the radiator.

Her pulse thudded in her neck, the *whoomph-whoomph* of it sounding loud in her head. She turned her back on it and faced the sink to the left. A mask hung from the tap by a white elastic strap with smears of brown on it—dried blood?

A female face with dark lips.

Jesus Christ.

She made the tea and returned to the living room with it. Handing it to him, she stepped back after he'd taken the cup.

"Why have you got a mask and wig in your kitchen?" she asked.

The cup fell from his hand and cracked on the laminate flooring, tea spilling and spreading.

"Not mine."

"Oh, does someone else live here with you then?"

"No."

"Then it must be yours. Getting it out ready for a fancy-dress party, were you?" *Trip yourself up, you bastard.* "And Halloween has already gone, so it can't be that. Can't say I like trick or treating myself. Got a bit sick of always being handed sticks of rock when I was kid. I bet everyone cleared Den out buying it from his shop."

"No." This time it was a low moan of a word, and he clutched his head, digging his fingertips in until his knuckles whitened.

Was it the mention of the rock?

"Then there's all those bloody *witches*," she said. "And those people walking around with knives, fake blood, the lot. It's enough to look like a load of *murderers* trotting about, isn't it?"

"Leave," he said.

"In a sec. Before we go, are you sure you don't know Felicity Greaves?"

"No."

"No, you're not sure, or no, you don't know her?" If she pissed him off enough, he might crack.

"Don't know her."

"I'll just clean up that tea for you," she said, dashing out to get a tea towel. A knife under it. A long, clean blade, the handle stained dark. *Oh my God…* Back in the living room, her heart thumping, she said, "That's a nice knife you have on your worktop, Ian."

He whipped his head round to stare at her. "I didn't tell you my name."

Shit.

"Oh, I'm sure you did. The knife. Where did you get it? I could do with one of those for cutting up liver and kidneys." She stared at him, waiting for him to catch on to the significance. "Do you like fish and chips? Den liked it. That was the last thing he had for his dinner, you know. What about spaghetti Bolognese? Mark had that." She sounded nonchalant, but inside she was tense. She was goading him but had no idea where to take it next.

He didn't seem to be all there.

A few Bibles short of a prayer meeting.

He faced the window again. "Go away now."

"The killer left evidence behind," she said casually. "We'll be swabbing all males in Smaltern next." *Liar.* "And we'll soon catch him. Would you like to give your swab now? It'll save us coming back and bothering you later, won't it."

"No."

"Okay, not a problem. Can you just answer my questions, though, then we'll leave you be. Why have you got a mask and wig in your kitchen, and where did you get that knife from?"

"Eddie gave me the mask and wig. The knife was Mum's."

"Fair enough." She glanced around the room, and her stomach clenched a few times. Sticking out from behind the sofa was a roll of plastic. "You know you said you were at home the night Mark and Den were killed? I'm just wondering… Why are you on CCTV walking along the alley beside his shop carrying a roll of plastic, much like the one you have down there?"

CHAPTER TWENTY

He was going to go mental in a minute if she didn't shut up. They knew it was him. She'd been gas-bagging it as though just making conversation, then had come out with that line about the wig and mask. Then the knife. The plastic. He'd known then that he didn't stand a chance so stood there trying to work out what to do next.

He remained focused on the front garden, waiting for an opportunity to leg it. The bloke copper leant on the living room wall. She stood in the doorway, and from the corner of his eye he caught her moving her jacket and flashing off one of those Tasers he'd seen on TV.

What, was she letting him know she'd use it?

He shrugged, as if that would make all of this go away.

"What's the matter, Ian? Got nothing to say?" she taunted.

He had plenty to say, just not to her. He had words sitting on his tongue, ready and waiting to be spoken to Benny, the next one on his list, but it didn't look like he'd be finishing the plan now.

That copper last night had fucked it all up.

"Is he dead?" he asked, cursing himself for opening his mouth.

"Who?" the Stratton woman asked.

"Doesn't matter." He needed the mask and wig. That would give him courage. He'd be able to cope then. At the moment, he felt like he had as a kid, lost under Eddie's influence, unable to make a proper decision. "I need to go and get a glass of water."

"Fine. I'll come with you," she said.

She needed to fuck right off. She was doing his head in.

Once she'd moved to the side, he walked past her and went to the kitchen. He lunged forward to grab the mask off the tap, her footsteps clicking on the hallway flooring. He slid the mask on, and instant calm came over him. Then he swiped the knife up and turned to face her, ready to stab her guts to pieces, slice up her liver and kidneys. Yeah, he knew what she'd been getting at when she'd said that.

She deployed the Taser, and the volts hit him square in the gut. The knife went flying, coming to rest in front of the cooker. He doubled over, body jerking, and fell to the floor on his side. He shook, then the wicked bite of the Taser wore off, and he stared at the knife, winded. He just needed a moment to compose himself, then he'd reach out for the blade and get her.

The man came in and, much as Ian tried to move, he couldn't; his body seemed paralysed. His hands were wrenched behind him by the bloke, the cuffs cold as they snapped into place.

"Ian Landon, you are under arrest…"

"No," he said, his voice coming out as his other self, the one who was stronger and able to cope. It was the mask, giving him strength, turning him into someone else. Someone important.

"…for the suspected murders of…"

Shut up. The man needed to shut up.

The woman stared at him, her eyes steely, but she didn't frighten him. He was strong. He was *somebody* now.

"I am Bête Noir," he said.

He laughed then, the trill of it maniacal, and his body filled with euphoria. She stared at him as though he were a prize, something she'd been looking for all her life. He'd made it. He'd got what he wanted.

Someone was taking notice of him.

"...Felicity Greaves, Den Simons, Mark Simons, and Katy Watkins. You have the right..."

The man droned on.

Then silence.

"You forgot the others," Bête said, cracking up, his breath from the laughter creating condensation on the inside of the mask and wetting his face.

"What others?" Stratton asked, panic tingeing her voice.

Got you there, haven't I, bitch?

"Wouldn't you like to know," Bête said.

He stared at her, hard, and she took a step forward.

"You're scum," she said. "Nothing but a piece of shit."

Eddie had told him that once, and those words hurt him, sent him back *there*, where he'd been insignificant and worthless.

His amusement died in an instant.

He was Ian again.

And he pissed himself.

CHAPTER TWENTY-ONE

Helena had left Landon in a holding cell for a few hours. He could fucking stew. Before two of the uniforms had transported him back to the station, he'd guffed on about his wig, saying he needed it to feel calm, that the mask alone wasn't helping.

"Did you wear that when you killed people?" she'd asked.

"What do you think, you silly cow?"

The sound of his voice had been weird. And as for the lady in the street, it had been him all along. Why he'd killed them all wasn't something he'd told her yet, and she hoped he would during the interview.

A forensic team were at his house now, sifting through everything. The poor sods had been at it for hours. Still, they all pulled together in times like these, working as one unit, just different branches of the same tree.

She got up from her desk and stared through the window, tired out from the adrenaline and just coming down from the high. It had been a mad few days, two cases back to back, and hopefully Smaltern would return to its usual sleepy self now.

People walked towards town on paths soaked by yet another recent downpour, although the wind wasn't as aggressive. The tail end of that hurricane hadn't stayed for long then.

She sighed and walked into the incident room. Louise had not long rung to say Landon's solicitor was here. Helena had asked for Doctor Varley to check Landon as soon as he'd arrived. She didn't want the little bastard claiming he wasn't fit for an interview. Varley had cleared him.

"Let's go then, Andy," she said, clapping him on the back.

He rose from his desk chair and let out a deep breath. "Wonder what bullshit excuse he's going to give?"

"If any."

"Going down for a long stretch, that one. Wouldn't surprise me if he didn't get to see outside the walls of a prison again." He stroked his chin.

"Consecutive life sentences, most likely."

"It's what he deserves," Ol said from across the room. "Actually, no, he doesn't deserve three square meals and a bloody PlayStation in his cell."

"Are you all right, Ol? Really?" Helena asked. "I don't want you here if you're upset. Do you want to go home?"

"No. I need to be at work." Ol smiled sadly. "Thanks anyway, though."

"We'll go out after work for a bevvy, shall we?" Helena asked. "All of us."

"Including us?"

Fuck. Helena turned around. Yarworth stood in the doorway with a bloke beside him. How could she say no without sounding a cow?

"If you like," she said grudgingly.

Someone let out a breath behind her. Probably Phil at the thought of having to spend time with the chief again.

"Team," Yarworth said, as if he was a part of it, "this is Evan Ufford. He'll be joining us next month some time, depending on when the current case he's working on is over. Kid gone missing, isn't it, Evan."

"It is." Evan smiled at everyone. "Hello."

The team returned his greeting, and Helena stood there awkwardly, not knowing what to say.

"Looking forward to working with you," she managed. *Think of how you'd feel in his shoes.* "Are you a beer or spirit man?"

"Bit of both," Evan said, smiling.

"Then we'll see you at the local about five," she said. "Sorry to cut this short, but we've got someone to interview."

"Oh?" Yarworth said, raising his eyebrows.

"We apprehended the killer earlier," she said and raised hers, too.

"Why didn't you tell me?" Yarworth asked.

She could tell the truth in front of Evan or lie. The truth won. "Because you told me never to bother you with that sort of thing, sir, until it was all tied up with a pretty bow. I think those were your words anyway."

Yarworth blushed and cleared his throat.

Evan hid a smile behind his hand and looked at Helena, eyes twinkling.

They'd get along fine.

"See you both later then?" she said, walking towards the exit.

"I'll… I'll give it a miss actually," Yarworth said.

I bet you bloody will.

"That's a shame. Phil, let Evan know where we'll be, will you?"

"Yes, guv."

Helena strode out and waited for Andy downstairs.

He grinned at her and shook his head. "You don't half know how to push your luck."

"Well, he shouldn't be such a dickhead, should he. Honestly, what's the point of pretending to be a DCI to show off for the new bloke when Evan's going to find out Yarworth is an office hermit who does jack shit? Christ."

"True."

Helena moved to the front desk. "Hi, missus. Are they ready for us?"

Louise nodded. "Yes, and what a creepy-looking fucker he is. Room two."

"Thanks."

Helena went in first. Landon sat on the left-hand side of the table, his solicitor next to him. A uniform stood in the corner. Helena sat in front of Landon, and the sound of the door closing gave her the shudders. She didn't like the expression on Landon's face. Andy took the seat beside her, and she touched his foot with hers and gave him a look—the look they shared when she was uneasy and needed to know he had her back. He nodded, but only just enough for her to catch it, then she faced forward.

She glanced up at the camera, and a red light came on. They were good to go.

She stated the date, time, the charges, her name, Andy's, the officer's, and Landon's, then, "And the solicitor present is…?"

"Tim Huxley." Youngish, brown hair, a pair of black specs, and stubble.

"Thank you."

"Ian, as you're already aware, you've been charged with four counts of murder. Felicity Greaves, Mark Simons, Den Simons, and Katy Watkins. Your roll of plastic, knife, wig, and mask have been taken by forensics and will undoubtedly throw up the DNA of the victims as well as yourself. It's pointless denying anything, so please, save us the hassle if you're thinking of going down the 'no comment' route."

He stared directly at her, his strange, unsettling eyes giving her the creeps.

"Now," she said, forcing herself to appear in control, although she didn't feel it. He bothered her in a way she couldn't explain. "You mentioned in your home that we 'forgot the others'. I took that to mean there are more people you've killed. Elaborate on that."

"No one important," he said in that eerie voice he'd slipped into earlier.

"Why are you speaking like that?" she asked.

"I'm pretending I have the mask on."

What? "Please explain that to me. Why do you need to pretend you have it on?"

"It calms me. Makes me feel safe. Important."

"Why do you need to feel important, Ian?"

"Because I never was."

"I see. Sorry about that." She wasn't, but if she could feign empathy, she might get more out of him. "Who weren't you important to?"

"Everyone."

"Give me some names."

"Mum, Dad, Eddie, Mark — and he was meant to be my friend and all. Den. He didn't like me. Probably because I used to nick his fags and saw him snogging my mum. Stupid bastard."

"Anyone else?"

"Them women you said about."

"Felicity and Katy?"

"Yeah."

While she'd gathered who Eddie was, she wanted him to clarify it. "Who is Eddie?"

Landon sat up straighter and rocked back and forth. "Bad things…bad things…"

"What do you mean by that?" she queried.

"He said bad things would happen, and they did." Landon hugged himself and stared at her, those bloody eyes of his narrow and piggy.

"What bad things?"

"You get killed. That's the bad thing. Eddie said not to tell."

"Tell me about Eddie."

"He was my mum's bloke."

"Where is Eddie now?"

"In the sea." He grinned like he had at his house and let out a strange little titter.

It put the shits up Helena, and Andy shifted in his seat. So he was feeling it, too. Thank God it wasn't just her imagination. Landon wasn't right in the head.

"Did you put him there?" she asked.

"Yeah."

"What about your mother? Where is she?"

"Ashes."

"How did she die?"

"Got run over by a train."

"I'm terribly sorry about that." *For her, not you.*

"I put her on the track." He giggled again, a high-pitched flutter of sound.

Jesus... "Okay, what about your dad?"

"I didn't kill him. He left us."

"Was that upsetting for you?" She imagined him as a child, left with his mother, feeling abandoned.

"Yeah. She got pissed after. Was always pissed." A mad glint sparkled in his eyes.

Fucking hell...

"Was she a good mother, though, Ian?"

"No."

"And what about Eddie? Was he good?"

"No." Back to that bland monotone.

"Has your mask fallen off?" She watched for his reaction.

He raised his hands and mimed putting it back on.

Dear God...

"What about your wig?" She swallowed.

He glanced about as if looking for it, then reached across the table in front of Andy and drew the invisible wig towards him. Ian put it on.

She had to wrap this up. Dr Varley had been wrong. This man wasn't mentally fit to be questioned. If she was any judge, he wouldn't be spending time in a regular prison.

"I just want to confirm, for the video, that you admit to killing the following people, okay?"

"Yeah." He straightened the wig; he must have thought it was slipping.

She almost felt sorry for him. "Regina Landon, Eddie Goddard, Felicity Greaves, Mark Simons, Den Simons, Katy Watkins. Please state your answer verbally."

"Yeah, they had the bad thing happen. Benny was meant to be next."

Jesus Christ. Phil's brother? Close call.

He stroked his face. Was he touching the rubber of the imaginary mask? Was his mind so broken he actually *felt* it? "But you got two the wrong way round. Eddie was first, then Regina."

"Thank you, Ian." She wasn't sure what to bloody think here. "Interview suspended at—"

"Can I have my knife back?" he asked, slowly tilting his head and glaring at her, his eyes piercing, frightening.

"No," she said.

Landon shot to his feet and looked down at the table, eyes wide as though he'd spotted something. Quicker than anyone could react, he swiped nothing into his hand and lunged across, forming a fist, and he brought it down as though holding a knife.

"One," he said in that freaky voice.

The side of his fist didn't make contact with the target of her stomach—Andy and the solicitor gripped Landon's arm at the same time, and the officer in the corner ran over and cuffed Landon's wrists behind him.

Landon blinked, staring at Helena's belly. He frowned. "You're not bleeding."

"That's enough, guys," she said. "Mr Landon needs a mental evaluation. I'm no longer prepared to continue." She signed off for the video and left the room, ushering a fearful-looking Tim Huxley out into the corridor.

"Fucking hell," Huxley said, leaning against the wall and staring at the ceiling.

Helena closed the door. "It's best we move into reception. The officer in there will be taking Landon back to holding in a second. I'm sure you don't really want to see him again just yet. Come on. I'll get you a cuppa."

She led him to the front desk, and he pressed his hands to it and hung his head. Louise widened her eyes, and Helena shook her head to stop her saying anything, then went to the vending machine. Andy came through, waved, and went upstairs.

"Tea or coffee, Mr Huxley?" she called over her shoulder.

"Um, tea. Please."

She pushed coins in and made the selection. Carrying the beige plastic cup over—Jesus, it was burning her fingers—she placed it on the desk. "Green, are you?" she asked.

"Clearly."

She smiled. "I've dealt with worse. You'll get used to it."

"I suppose I'll have to."

Helena patted his shoulder then made her way to the incident room. Although what Landon had done had rattled her, as had his eyes, his smile, his weird voice, she couldn't let that stop her elation. She'd thought there were two killers and she'd only found one in Landon. It had bugged her no end, but it didn't matter.

No. She'd finally found the lady in the street.

Printed in Great Britain
by Amazon

47749734R00148